A Pineville Easter

ANNE FONS

Cover designed by Valdas Miskinis

Anne Fons
Visit my website at www.AnneFons.com

Printed in the United States of America

First Printing: March 2019
Anne Fons Readers Group

ISBN-13 978-1-0909508-7-1

This book is dedicated to my father,
Medard Fons,
who was, and is, my hero.
May you look down from heaven and know
you are always
a part of my heart.
I love you, Daddy.

Also, for Jason
& Basil,
whose favorite holiday is Easter.

∞ ∞ ∞

Chapter One

Her teenage brother stared her straight in the eyes. His tone was challenging. "Why don't you just admit you want to get me out of Milwaukee? Admit that you don't want me to hang around with my friends."

It bothered Julia that Jeremy felt so miserable. Yet, she knew that getting him into a new environment somewhere she could have help with raising him was the best answer, at least for now. "Maybe we can move back in a year or so."

"Yeah, sure."

Julia looked around her. The Southwest side of Milwaukee was decidedly a working person's part of town. There was nothing flashy about it and nothing run down either. People kept their houses maintained, their cars in repair and their sidewalks shoveled. She had lived in this area for all of her life. It was comfortable. It was home.

She blinked and shook away the shudder that suddenly enveloped her. Jeremy wasn't the only one who would miss this place.

Gazing upward, she noticed some late winter clouds forming in the sky. Living in the Midwest gives one a real feel for what snow clouds look like, and Julia was certain that growing mass of light gray was full of the slippery white stuff.

She glanced at the few odds and ends still sitting on the front porch, waiting to somehow get loaded into the compact car.

Her nerves were already frayed from the recent stress of her grandmother's passing and then the decision to move. Adding icy roads to the mix would not help.

Jeremy continued his argument. "First, I lose my parents. Then, my grandma, and now you want to take me away from my friends! You just don't care how I feel. Do you?"

Julia found enough of her voice to speak slightly above a whisper. "You know that's not true, Jeremy."

His tone became mocking. "Do I?"

The same tone, the same arguing, they were two of the factors that led to Julia reaching out to her grandmother's brother, their only remaining relative, for some help. She prayed that the small-town minister had all the wisdom that she didn't feel she had herself.

"Look, your friends, I don't think they're bad kids. I really don't, but I do think they are making some really foolish choices lately. One of these days, if they don't figure it out, they are going to get themselves into actual trouble. I don't want you with them when that happens."

"You worry about everything."

"Maybe, but I am the one that needs to worry about all this."

"I think it's easy for you to blame me for stuff. You are afraid to have a good time. You know that? All you want is for everybody to live in the little perfect 'Julia' world. Well, I don't intend to grow up to be a monk or a minister like Uncle

Wilbur, living in some town that nobody knows. So, let me live my life my way. I won't blame you if I turn out to be a bum. At least I will be a bum that has fun."

She turned away from him then and headed toward the driver's side of the car. "Please get the other things from the porch and put those quilts on the top. We should get going. It's over three hours to Pineville, and that's without any more snow. I promised Uncle Wilbur we would be there in time for supper."

"Why can't you pack the car yourself? You're the one who wants to move. I just get stuck with all the work."

Julia climbed into the car and rested her hands and her head momentarily on the steering wheel. She knew this wasn't going to be easy. A car accident took their parents when Jeremy was only seven years old. Though Grandma Margaret's passing was only a few months ago, Julia could already sense she was going under taking care of her brother on her own. Sixteen wasn't an easy age. Adding these circumstances certainly wouldn't make it easier. She wondered how Grandma Margaret took care of the both of them for all those years and made it look so effortless. Then again, Grandma Margaret had experience with parenting. Julia didn't.

Jeremy slammed the trunk shut and followed that by slamming the passenger door. He was consistent, in his tone, in his defensiveness, in his actions.

Julia tried to pat him on the shoulder, but he shrugged her kindness away.

Instead he turned to her with the same irritated look on his face. "So, tell me again why we can't just stay in this house? Grandma it to us."

"Jeremy, it costs a lot to keep a house in shape, not to mention the taxes."

"Yeah, well, you're not selling it. So, you still have all of that stuff, to," he inserted air-quotes into the space between them, "worry about."

Julia took a deep breath. "I told you. Stephanie's brother is renting the place. He'll look after it for now. If I still can't handle the expenses, then we'll sell it."

"Great," Jeremy said. With that, he put in his ear buds, cranked up his music to a volume about one step shy of blowing out his eardrums and positioned himself for sleep.

Julia started the ignition and with one last look at the house that had been her home for many years, she pulled away from the curb.

Chapter Two

The noise that Jeremy called music started wearing on Julia's nerves.

It was another reminder of the distance that had recently grown between them. It hurt her to know that he wasn't the little boy that would tell her everything anymore. It's not that she wanted to know about his private life, but she wished he would include her in his concerns. No one should need to try to navigate the teen years without guidance and not the guidance of other sixteen-year-old boys. He needed an adult's help. Maybe he would open up more to their great-uncle. She sure wasn't the one to whom he was reaching out these days.

She turned on her own music to keep her company on the drive and get her mind off the challenges she was facing. She had spent more than enough time dwelling on that and there was sure to be plenty more time for it later. The first song that came on was a love song, another one followed. By that second song, Julia knew she needed to switch to something more up-tempo. Love songs were not going to help right now either.

There was no way she could fit a romantic love into her present life. Jeremy needed her, and she would make sure he turned out ok if it took every last ounce of her patience that remained.

The cityscape of Milwaukee faded into that of the sprawling suburbs as Julia made her way west on I-94. She liked some of these places, and was glad Jeremy was asleep for the moment. She knew he would remind her how much she enjoyed driving this way on a Sunday afternoon, meeting her best friend, Stephanie, for coffee at one of the many little places out this way. She didn't need to be reminded of how much she would miss Steph or that time together. It was her favorite time of the week.

Stephanie was a dreamer and a chatterbox. She saw a half-full crystal glass with a cherry spritzer when Julia saw a disposable cup with lukewarm tea and a possible leak. There was nothing that kept her friend down.

Stephanie's Sunday 'mocha-with-whip' came with musings of who would be the perfect man for each of them, plus stories about her two-dozen kindergarteners. Stephanie may not as yet have found her perfect soulmate, but she had found the perfect career for herself. Putting energetic, fun-loving and imagination-encouraging Stephanie with five-and-six-year-olds was about as natural a fit as a custom-made shoe.

Sunday's coffee conversations always began with a 'medium-decaf-with-skim' on Julia's side of the table. She loved listening to Stephanie dream about what life could hold for each of them. As for herself, Julia had found neither perfect fit and doing so was not on her radar. While Stephanie dreamed of a handsome hero sweeping her off her feet in romance, Julia talked of Jeremy's grades and attitudes. While Stephanie talked about the latest art project or a kindergartener sticking straws up his nose in the lunchroom, Julia's were replete with stories of hard-to-find downtown parking spaces and broken copy machines. Her job as an office clerk at an insurance agency was fine but didn't bring the same hilarity to the conversation as twenty-four rambunctious kindergarten kids. Since Julia didn't spend any after-work hours socializing, her co-workers were just that, not close friends. That was ok with her. Julia always preferred quality to quantity, and she had the best friend she could possibly have in Stephanie.

They had been friends their entire lives growing up a couple houses apart when they were little and a couple of blocks apart when Julia and Jeremy went to live with Grandma Margaret.

She prayed as she drove that she had made the right decision. Not atypical for Julia, she found herself repeatedly rethinking it on her office breaks, at lunch, while making dinner and while trying to fall asleep. If it had not been for Stephanie telling her that enough was enough, and to, "Call your uncle now, not after you've slept on it one more night," she would probably still be tossing and turning at night deciding what to do.

She trusted Stephanie's judgement. She trusted her great-uncle's. Now, she needed to trust that somehow, the little town of Pineville and its people, would be the place where her younger brother would find his happiness again.

Suburban scenery melted away to the Lake Country area. It was too early in the year for people to be boating and too late for ice fishing. The quiet waters on either side of her car reminded her that there were places not so hectic as a large city. She loved her hometown, but right now, she was ready for some peace and quiet.

By the time she passed from the lake area to the rolling farmland, Julia found herself thinking about all the positive things this new home could entail. Quiet nights with a good book, weekend days walking down Main Street meeting new people, and Jeremy finding the right group of friends at his new school. Uncle Wilbur said there were many nice people in Pineville, and to her knowledge, her great-uncle was rarely wrong.

After taking the I-94 turn to the north outside of Madison, the clouds that had threatened snow earlier in the day began to fulfill their promise as big fluffy snowflakes descended on to the road. By the time they reached Wisconsin Dells, the wind blew, and the pretty white flakes were getting less pretty and more dense.

Julia slowed her driving and watched for her turnoff. Once she was on the local highway toward Pineville, the snow became thicker yet again. It was also getting deeper. She was grateful to see a flashing orange light and followed behind a county snowplow as she switched her wipers to high speed and looked for a place to stop and wait out the passing squall.

The snowplow driver turned into a large parking lot just off the highway. The substantial-size log building had a lighted sign, "Pineville Diner and Campground."

She pulled into what she thought was a parking space and shut off the engine. "Food stop," she said as she gently shook Jeremy's arm.

"I thought you said we were eating at Uncle Wilbur's house tonight," he said.

"We will, but the weather's crummy, and I really didn't eat much yet today. Let's get something light, wait out the bulk of this snow and then get back on the road. I think we are only a couple of miles away now."

"So, why don't you keep driving? You've driven in snow before, Julia."

"I know," Julia said. "I just need to stop for a bit. I want to make sure I have the right directions from here. With the snow coming down this heavy, it's really getting hard to see any kind of road signs."

"Fine," Jeremy replied with a terse tone. "I don't need to get to 'nowhere' anytime soon anyway."

Chapter Three

Julia and Jeremy stomped the snow off their boots and brushed the large flakes of snow from their hair as they walked into the diner. The log walls held old black-and-white pictures, many dating back over one-hundred years. The cut-out windows were framed in cheerful gingham-checked curtains. Customers in jeans, plaid flannel shirts and trucking-company caps dotted the open room. The occasional laughter and convivial chatting at the tables were as welcoming as the waitress's greeting. "Hi there! Grab a table, folks. Be with you in a moment."

The two slid into a green vinyl booth that had the color of pine needles and the wear of years. The table looked like split logs that were topped with enough varnish to withstand puddles of dripped maple syrup and mounds of gooey strawberry jam. Everything was polished, comfortable and definitely not from the city.

Julia handed a menu to Jeremy and then took one for herself. "What looks good?" she asked as she started to scan it.

"Not this place," muttered Jeremy.

Lucas Anderson couldn't stop the look he gave the boy. He knew the type. Giving him a quick look over, he confirmed his own first impression. Tennis shoes sporting the name of a pro basketball player. Never had to work to earn the money. Haircut that looked like he belonged on an expensive skateboard. Gets everything he wants. That smirk on his face. Cocky. Spoiled. Had the world handed to him. The list in his mind could go on for a long time.

He glanced at the young woman sitting across from him. What was wrong with her? She was too old to be his date and too young to be his mother. The kid was too old to need a babysitter, but he sure needed someone to make him tow the line.

Julia saw the glare Lucas gave her brother. She wondered if he had overheard Jeremy's snide comment. She looked at the man and ventured a small, stiff smile. Instead of smiling back, the look he returned to her was one of disgust. Julia knew her brother's comment wasn't nice, but she didn't think it warranted that type of behavior from this man. This stranger knew nothing of what her brother was going through in his life. "Well, thankfully," Julia said to no one in particular, "we'll never have to see him again."

"Coffee?" Jeannie asked with the pot in her hand.

"Yes, please," Julia replied as she smiled at the friendly waitress.

"Chocolate shake," Jeremy said without looking up from his menu.

Jeannie poured Julia's coffee and came back with the shake for Jeremy. "What else can I get for you folks today?" she asked.

Jeremy replied, "Cheeseburger and fries."

Julia looked at the menu one more time. "What would you suggest?" she asked. "We're having supper at my uncle's in a bit, but something small would be good."

"Your uncle from around here?" Jeannie asked.

"Yes, he lives in this town."

"If he lives in Pineville, I probably know him."

"His name is Wilbur Plain."

"Well, I'll be," Jeannie said. "You're the reverend's grandniece moving here from Milwaukee." She looked over at Jeremy, "And this must be your brother. Welcome to Pineville!"

"I guess you do know my uncle," Julia laughed.

"Honey," the waitress said, "this is a small town. It's hard not to know each other, let alone the church minister."

Jeannie looked outside at the swirling snow. "Well," she said to Julia, "given the weather outside, and your supper being soon, how about a bowl of homemade soup? Don made some beef vegetable today, and it's mighty good."

"Perfect," Julia said. "Is Don the chef?"

Jeannie chuckled. "Chef, owner – and my husband. Plus, he makes a great pot of soup."

Once the waitress had left the table, Julia spoke to Jeremy. "So, this is our last stop before we get to Uncle Wilbur's and our new home. Is there anything you want to talk to me about, or ask me about, before we get there?"

Jeremy pulled out his cell phone. "Nope," he said as he switched his concentration from his sister sitting across from him to the technology in his hand.

Since her brother was engrossed in his phone, Julia took some time to study all there was to see in the Pineville Diner. From the log-style tables to the gingham curtains which set a pretty frame around the snow-dotted windows, everything fit. Even the people. Soft country music filtered off and on through the myriad of conversations. She noticed again how everyone seemed to have a nice time talking and visiting with each other, grandparents and grandbabies, moms and dads, truckers and whomever else happened to come into the place that day, like her and Jeremy.

The smile that had been on Julia's face faded a little. Jeremy. She let out a small sigh. He was still engrossed in his phone and not one of the happy people here at the Pineville Diner.

Yet, Julia knew her nice kid brother was still inside the brooding teenager. She was open to trying anything Uncle Wilbur might suggest regarding getting her brother back to his former happy self. She had tried, but on her own, she didn't seem to have the right words. He's a minister, Julia thought. He will know what to say and do.

"Here you go, folks!" Jeannie said as she brought the food to the table. She placed the soup in front of Julia.

"Oh, wow! That smells good!" Julia said.

"Best in town," said Jeannie. "Don makes a fresh soup every day. You'll have to stop by again and try another one."

"I'd love to," said Julia. "This looks incredible!"

Jeannie put a plate in front of Jeremy. The burger was big, and the fries were piled high and filled out the plate to the very edges. "I'd ask you if you thought you could eat a dinner after this," the waitress said, "but I have five kids, three of which were at one time teenage boys. They never met a meal they couldn't finish," she said with a slight laugh.

She turned back to Julia. "I'm Jeannie, by the way. No doubt you'll be seeing plenty of me at the church, and I really do hope you'll come back to the diner again. You seem like a sweet person, and your Uncle Wilbur is so happy to have you both here! He even reminded us after services last week."

"Thank you," Julia said. "I definitely will come back." She extended her hand. "I'm Julia, and this is my brother, Jeremy."

"Nice to meet you, too, Jeremy," Jeannie said. "Some of the kids come out here to study once in awhile. You're always welcome."

Jeremy looked up from his food. "I'm not much of a study group person but thank you."

"Well, like I said," Jeannie said, "you're always welcome if you want to come around."

Chapter Four

"I'm sorry Jeremy didn't stay to talk after dinner, Uncle Wilbur," Julia said. "I guess he wanted to let all of his friends know we got here ok."

They walked along a path that led from the parsonage around the perimeters of the church property. The snow was falling lightly now, and the winds had died down, making it a pleasant evening for an early stroll. They walked slowly to keep their feet from slipping and to take their time with each other and the conversation. It seemed that Uncle Wilbur, Reverend Plain, did many things at a slow pace, including walking and talking. Yes, he had girth and age to him, but Julia suspected that wasn't why. She felt he would have taken his time with anything, even as a younger, and thinner, man. Julia noticed there was often a break between her sentences and his.

"Perhaps," the reverend said. "Tell me, Julia, have things with Jeremy gotten any better at all since we last spoke?"

Julia shook her head. "No. Worse actually. He's convinced I moved him here to get him away from his friends."

"We both know he's not wrong about that."

"No, I mean, well, but that's not the only reason. There's the house, and the bills and oh, Uncle Wilbur. I just want him to be happy, the way he used to be."

"There's no 'just' about that, Julia. That's a tall order. Not unattainable, of course, but not necessarily something that will happen in a snap.

Her great-uncle continued. "Moving here might help him. We will need to see."

"Pineville seems so nice," Julia said. "Grandma Margaret always loved to come here. To use her expression, she said the people were some of, 'God's best'."

"Good people are in all places, Julia. Pineville is one of them. You will meet many wonderful people here who will help you in any way they can and be there whenever you need them. It's small town living."

Julia smiled a little. "That sounds like what we need."

The reverend stopped for a moment. He looked around a bit at the church grounds, quiet and cloaked in its own tranquil beauty. He began walking again. "I definitely think coming to Pineville is right for you, Julia," he said.

Julia was a bit taken aback. "But not for Jeremy?" she asked.

"No, I'm not saying that. Jeremy may do very well here. That will be up to him. Only he can decide if he will warm to the hearts that are around him." He stopped talking for a moment. "You know, youth is an interesting time. Teenagers see so many things, and people, in one dimension. Right now, he sees that he wants to be with his friends, the ones he knows, even if down deep he knows that not everything they are doing is wise. You're the big sister, the one who wants to take him away from that."

"Those kids aren't the ones to whom he should turn for advice. I'm the one who is trying to help him."

"Yes, you are trying. They are, too, in their own ways."

"Do you think I am overreacting to this? I see him as unhappy."

"He is unhappy right now, and with some valid reasons. He lost his grandmother a few months ago, and now he also thinks he is losing his house, his neighborhood, his school, and his friends."

"Jeremy said some of those same things to me," Julia said, "except his had a different tone."

Reverend Plain gave a little laugh. "I am sure they did."

"So, what am I doing that I shouldn't?"

"Nothing."

"Well, what am I not doing that I should?"

"Nothing for now."

Julia looked up into her great-uncle's eyes. "How come you make it sound so easy? Grandma Margaret did that, too."

"Oh, Julia," Uncle Wilbur said, "it's not easy at all. It is simply the way life goes. We cannot make a plan for anyone else and expect them to fulfill it. We cannot fulfill it for them, either. Sometimes we have to have the incredible strength to let them find out for themselves if what we say is true."

They had come to the far edge of the church property. Before turning back, her great-uncle once again stopped and looked around at all there was to see. In those moments of pause, Julia saw his face relax and his eyes soften.

"Child," he said as they started back to the parsonage, "you cannot find happiness for anyone else. That is something they have to do, and discover, for themselves."

"And in the meantime?" Julia asked.

"Give him needed structure and boundaries, let him work at figuring it out, and be there if he falls."

"Uncle Wilbur, that doesn't sound very optimistic. You make it sound as though Jeremy will fail and there is nothing I can do to prevent that." She stopped along the walkway and kicked some snow off her boots.

Reverend Plain held his hand in the air. "First, Julia, I said 'if', not when. Second, should that happen, remember that we all fail at times in life. Sometimes we think we failed when in fact we really didn't."

He brought his hand back down to his side. "Your brother is headstrong. Yes, that may get him into some trouble of sorts at times, but it may also help him get out of it. It all depends on which directions he decides to take. Another thing for you to remember, Julia, is that he has his own compass. You cannot force him to go into any particular direction, but you can point the way by setting the best example you can for him. Hopefully, over a fairly short period of time, he will see that is a better way to live."

"I'm not used to letting go of him. I worry."

"Yes, I understand. Margaret saw it, and I do, too."

"I'm not sure how to do that."

"You need to find a way to focus on other parts of life in addition to Jeremy. For example, that new job you are starting tomorrow."

Julia kicked snow from her boots again. She wiped the top of her boot that came from a small drift that had accumulated on a tiny slope of the footpath.

"I am really looking forward to working at the church with you, Uncle Wilbur," she said. "Oh, by the way, do you want me to call you Uncle Wilbur or Reverend Plain when we are there?"

"I'm your uncle. Let's go with that unless there are parishioners around that might not know who you are. We are pretty laid back here."

Julia took in the property that housed the old clapboard church, the small historic cemetery, the bungalow parsonage, the playground and the field beyond. "Pineville is idyllic. It's a perfect new start."

Reverend Plain shook his head and gently waved his finger to caution his grand-niece. "Oh, nothing is perfect, even Pineville."

Seeing Julia's sudden wariness, he broke into a smile, "But, we're close."

When they reached the back door of the parsonage, Julia once again started scraping ice and snow from the top of her boots to keep it from seeping through to her ankles. "Do you have a caretaker who shovels this for you, Uncle Wilbur, or can I do it for you?"

"Well, some of the kids and the dads from the congregation often stop by to do it, but I told the council I have someone new to do it for me for the rest of the season."

Julia recognized that she was the new church secretary, and in a small community church, she would probably have ample time to shovel the walk as well as her other duties. "I'll get right on that," she said as she picked up the shovel from its spot on the porch next to the kitchen door.

Wilbur took the shovel from her hands. "No, you are the secretary, and with us in the busy Lenten season, you will have plenty to do inside the church."

He held the door open for her to enter. "Jeremy," he called.

Jeremy came into the kitchen.

"I need you to take care of shoveling the walk tonight. Since your sister and I made the meal and did the dishes, I think we've earned a rest and a cup of hot tea."

Jeremy glared at Julia as he passed her, grabbing his jacket from the peg near the kitchen door. He took the shovel from his great-uncle's hands and closed the door just a little harder than was necessary on the way outside.

Later that evening, Julia crawled into bed, nestled under her quilt that Grandma Margaret had made for her when she was a child. The soft pinks and lavenders of the petals and the delicate yellow centers in the Dresden Plate style quilt always made her remember her grandmother's softness, her soothing voice and how love came through everything she did, including her beautiful quilts.

The soothing voice was gone now, but the soft, pretty fabric was still there, reminding her how much she was loved, and how much her grandmother did to make both hers and Jeremy's lives still feel safe and comforted, even in the aftermath of their parents' deaths.

Feeling pangs of sadness and needing to let out the day's highs and lows, Julia called her best friend. The sounds of Stephanie's cheerful voice and ebullient laughter always could brighten her day.

"Hi, Steph," she said.

"Hey, best friend. How was the drive? Are you settled at your uncle's? How's Bro-Bro doing?" Stephanie always asked a litany of questions.

Julia wondered how she could do that all in one breath. "Well," she said, "we're here."

"Good," said Stephanie. "Safe drive? Any problems with the snow? We had some squalls move through Milwaukee a little bit ago."

"The drive was pretty decent. We made a stop at a diner at the edge of town when that snow started blowing sideways." Julia took a sip of the tea she had brought upstairs with her. "You should see it, Stephanie. It's such a cute place, and the people there were really friendly." She curled her lip. "Well, most of them anyway. One guy was a real jerk."

"What did he do? Was he mean to his wife? Kids? You?"

Julia laughed. "Whoa, no need to call in the cavalry! First of all, I doubt that guy has a wife or kids. He is just unpleasant nasty. He gave Jeremy such a look! Thankfully, Jeremy was oblivious. His head in his phone as usual."

"Why would he do that? Do you think he doesn't like strangers? You said Pineville is a small place. Sometimes those people are pretty cliquish I've heard."

"No, I just think he has an attitude, thinks he has all the answers for the world. You know, the type that thinks everybody in the world should be just like them. He obviously judges people before he has one fat clue of what the other person's life is like."

"Well, he better not mess with my best friend, or I will be in pretty Pineville to put that guy in his place."

Julia smiled. "While I miss you already, and would love to see you, I don't think you need to make a special trip. Odds are I won't see him again. He was probably some trucker passing through who had an argument with his wife before he got here."

"I thought you said he wasn't husband material, Julia."

"He's not in my book, but I guess if someone is even remotely good-looking, someone will put up with their garbage."

Stephanie actually took a breath before responding. "Hold it, BFF. You never said he was good-looking. How good-looking is he?"

Julia let out a sound of exasperation. "Stephanie, that isn't the point. I don't care if he's as handsome as a movie star in the sunshine. I don't judge people by their looks, and you know it. He's just a rude guy that I hope never to see again."

"Yep. I hear you."

"Thank you."

"So, what color are his eyes?"

Chapter Five

Early spring rain greeted Julia on the first morning of her new job. "So like Wisconsin," she said as she took an umbrella from the stand near the kitchen door, "thirty degrees one day, fifty the next. At least this will wash most of the snow away."

She left the house early that day, even though she needed to walk only about a quarter of a block down the path. She liked getting places early, to get the feel of where she was, to take in everything she could before her day began.

Despite the steady drizzle, she stopped at the sign in front of the church. She read aloud. "Pineville Community Church. Services – Sunday, 10 a.m.. Sunday School – 9 a.m.. Reverend Wilbur Plain, Minister. Mrs. Myrtle Hodges, Secretary. Mr. Don Anderson, Organist." Julia took a breath. "Myrtle," she mused, "I hope I can fill your shoes." She chuckled. "And I guess the Pineville Diner Chef doubles as an organist."

"Oh, don't you worry about that sign, Miss," a man's voice said. "We'll be changing it to your name, as soon as Myrtle thinks it's a good idea."

Julia turned to see a short wiry man who looked to be in his sixties. "Oh, I am not worried about that. Mrs. Hodges can stay on that sign as long as she wants."

"She will."

"Um, ok. Is there a problem of which I should be aware?"

"No problem. Just Myrtle is Myrtle, and you ain't going to change her."

"I thought she wanted to retire," Julia said.

"She did. However, Myrtle Hodges has been the church secretary for thirty years. She knows God owns the place, but she thinks she comes in second to being in command."

"And Reverend Plain?" Julia asked.

"Well, he is the reverend and all, but Myrtle keeps the calendar and makes sure he gets wherever she thinks he ought to be. Reverend Plain, he doesn't mind. He'd get there anyway, but since Myrtle likes telling people what to do, he just lets her."

"I'm sorry, but I'm not sure this is my business. You can be certain that my unc- um, Reverend Plain will be fully in command while I am in the office."

"As long as Myrtle says so."

The man stuck out his hand to shake hers. "I'm sorry. I am forgetting my manners. We don't get too many new folks here in Pineville, and I just kind of get to thinking that everyone knows everyone else. I'm Deke Anderson."

"Another Anderson? Is everyone in this town related?" Julia asked.

"Nah, only about half of us." With that he laughed and walked up the steps to open the front door for her. "I guess

Myrt will give you a key later today," he said as he unlocked the front door."

"Thank you," she said as she stepped inside the old building.

"I'll just go grab the rest of my tools and such and be back with you in a minute. I'll give you the five-cent tour. Excuse me," he said as he went out to his truck.

Once inside the old church, Julia's senses were overcome with familiar sights, smells, touches, and a reverential silence. The entryway was filled with dark wood and deep red carpet, much like many other old parish buildings she had seen. Yet, though she had seen other interiors similar, Julia reached to touch the smooth, century-old wood. It felt protective in some way, as though many had gone before her here and had been welcomed into its warmth.

Julia's eyes took in the brass collection plates, with barely a tarnish mark among them. The insides were lined with red felt in an attempt to not only diminish the clanging of any coins that came into them on Sunday mornings, but also to vaguely match the carpeting. Julia smiled. The cheery red felt, coming up at the edges of the rounded offering plates, didn't quite match the somber deep ruby of the carpet. She made a mental note to find out what kind of glue to buy and recover the worn ones.

She moved slowly along the wall to the long brass lighting sticks. They were probably four-feet-high and designed to reach the higher candles that she saw through the open sanctuary doors. She felt the side of one and decided that someone in the Pineville church must have a fondness for them, as they gleamed with brightness.

She walked into the rear of the sanctuary itself. The pews were the same dark wood, and the carpet the same dark red. The purple vestments on the altar for the Lenten season, the tall candles, and the large stained-glass window depicting Jesus with a lamb, added to the mix with a royal, yet soft, feeling.

A list of yesterday's hymn numbers adorned the walls near the sanctuary entrance, permanent, dark wooden holders with slats for movable, numerical slate tiles. The modern churches Julia had seen no longer had things like those, either putting the hymn numbers in the bulletins or projecting them on a large screen. Julia liked this older way, the honoring of a tradition, yes, but more than that. Once again, she felt wrapped in a comfort of old, of the intimacy of a quiet old church.

She loved old buildings. She breathed deep. The smell of timeworn wood mixed with the fragrance of the withered carnations that were left from yesterday's service. Her eyes followed her senses.

Deke was coming back in the front door and noticed the carnations about a half-second after Julia. He scooped them from the chair where they had been laid and hastily stuck them inside his jacket.

Seeing the quizzical look on Julia's face, he said, "Myrtle will pitch a fit if she sees these flowers didn't get delivered to the nursing home yesterday. We take them there after services for the older people to enjoy. The staff there puts them in water, and they actually last quite a few days. You let them sit out here, just wrapped in cellophane like this, and they wilt overnight."

"Is that something the secretary normally does?"

"Only when it's her turn," Deke said. "Yesterday must have been Abe Wilder's. He's getting up in years himself, and he forgets a few things now and again.'

"And Myrtle wouldn't understand that Abe has difficulties?" Julia asked.

"She'd understand, sure, but she would watch him like a hawk from now until he draws his last breath. Poor guy would get reminded ten times before he left the building, and she'd probably call the home to make sure they were delivered.'

"Quite serious about her job, I guess that's an attribute, too," Julia replied.

Deke scratched his head. "You're a kind one."

He studied her face for a moment or two. "Hey, you were at the diner yesterday, weren't you?"

"Yes, my brother and I stopped there to wait out the snow squall. I haven't been in Pineville many times and didn't want to get turned around on these back roads. Frankly, the last time I was here I was about twelve or so. I don't remember much, just the river and the picnics on the church grounds."

"I thought I remembered your face – from yesterday of course, not from when you were twelve."

"Thank you. Are you one of the diner's chefs, too?"

"Nope. That honor goes to my brother and his wife. People wouldn't want to eat anything I would cook for them. On the other hand, they probably wouldn't want Jeannie helping them shingle their roofs or cutting timber."

Deke set his toolbox down near the top of the basement steps. "I run the campground side. Since this time of year is slow for me, I help at the church with whatever needs fixing, shoveling, or mowing. Donny can play the organ. I can fix a broken step. Watch that fourth one on your way down to the basement. It's got a little wiggle right now, but it will be sturdy as a telephone pole by the time I'm done with it."

He stopped and looked at her again. "Well, welcome to Pineville. You'll do fine here, and don't mind Myrtle. She's a good egg that comes across as a drill sergeant with the prickly heat. Oh, um, pardon me, ma'am. I spend my time around men too much. Once in awhile I forget how to talk to a lady."

She chuckled. "No worries, Mr. Anderson. I'll watch out for the wobbly step – and for Myrtle."

"Just call me Deke. I prefer it. There are too many titles in our family as it is."

"And I am Julia."

Julia walked to the little office on the left side of the hall, tucked under the steps leading up to the choir loft and organ. Having it be an office was definitely not part of the original architectural plan, but it was cozy and included a small, set-back stained-glass window of a dove and a heart that let the outside light filter a red and white glow through the space.

Everything here was tidy as a pin. Julia felt that Myrtle Hodges must also be a stickler for organization and cleanliness. She corrected herself. "You've never even met the woman," Julia softly said. "Don't make assumptions, Julia Beth."

She continued to scope out her new office. There were the basic necessities, a desk with a secretary's chair, a computer, a phone, a printer, and a couple of filing cabinets. They were not fancy or elaborate, but practical for the needs of the church. "Oh, look at these," she said to no one but herself as she saw a couple relics from the past in the manual typewriter and a mimeograph machine. The room was filled but organized. On the wall under the stairs hung a large whiteboard calendar, and a small cross-stitch of "The Lord's Prayer" was framed atop the tallest filing cabinet next to her desk. A mix of modern and traditional, Julia thought. She smiled and daydreamed about how much she could love this little space, an office of her own. It was so unlike the sterile cubicle she shared with three other women in her former workplace in downtown Milwaukee. She was lost in thought, imagining how sweet life could be here, how she would make this little space truly her own.

"You're the new secretary." A woman's voice, tough as nails, swept away her ease with few words and plenty of tone.

"Yes, Julia Garver. You must be Myrtle, or do you prefer Mrs. Hodges?"

"Either one will do. Let's get down to business. I've got a week to get you up to speed, and that won't be enough time to teach you the half of it. I've written down my home phone number on a piece of paper under the phone. Don't call unless you need me, though I expect that will happen often enough."

"Um, yes, ma'am," Julia said. Her voice was usually quite clear, but in Myrtle's presence she sounded like a junior high school student caught passing a note in class. She felt as if she had been reprimanded and warned at the same time.

"Ma'am's not necessary."

One thing was certain, Myrtle knew her job and was very good at it. She spent the first half of the morning showing Julia how to work the phone system, where to find the office supplies, and explaining the various duties she would perform on a regular basis. By ten a.m., Julia's head was spinning from trying to absorb all of it. The last thing she wanted to do was to ask Myrtle Hodges to explain it to her a second time.

"How old are you?" Myrtle asked.

"Twenty-five."

"I figured about that. Well, given your age, I don't suppose I need to show you how to work a computer. Do I?"

"No, unless you have special software for the church or something."

"Frankly, Miss Garver, I keep very little on that computer. I don't trust them. Typewriters and filing cabinets work just fine for me. The accounting items used to be done in a ledger until that upstart accountant from the Dells started demanding that we put it in a computer spreadsheet. Even though I showed them the completeness and usefulness of the handwritten ledgers, our church council gave in to the

CPA's 'request'. So, you will find the financials on the computer, and I started using it to make out the weekly bulletins a year or two ago. It does help quite a bit with anything repetitive, less typing means less time spent. However, most other correspondence is kept in the locked filing cabinets over there. Any questions?"

"I think I am ok for now."

"Good, take a break. The rain stopped. You might want to walk outside a bit to clear your head. We will get to the calendar later this morning, and then I have some errands to run the rest of the day. Gather all your questions as they come up this afternoon, and I will answer them in the morning."

"Thank you."

Yes, a walk was what she needed, thought Julia, a very long walk.

Despite wanting to run, not walk, as far away from Myrtle Hodges as she could, Julia was anxious to get on with work. She wanted to do what she had always done in the past, master the task, and do it well. She walked back in the office in less than fifteen minutes after she had left.

Myrtle checked her watch. "You're punctual. I like that. You were here before me this morning, and that's something few people ever do. You came back from your walk in a timely fashion. Now days, you never know with younger people. Some of them have no conception of work. They just want to mark time and collect a paycheck. Well, this is not a job that will make you rich, but it is richly rewarding."

"I don't intend to get rich," Julia said. "Rewarding is a word that's nice to hear."

"Don't pat yourself on the back too hard, Miss Garver. We have a lot more to go, but I will admit we are off to a good beginning."

"I will take that as a compliment."

"Fine," said Myrtle. "Are you ready for the calendar?"

"I think so."

"All right." Myrtle walked over to the immense whiteboard. She picked up a marker and pointed to each item as she explained her system to Julia. "Sundays are pretty self-explanatory. We have Sunday School, choir practice, and service. The council people on duty will do the counts for the day before they lock up. I tend to stay until they are done, but it is not required. Much of your Sundays will be spent assisting other people, congregants, ushers, council persons, the reverend, etc.. Just do what needs to be done."

Julia hadn't really considered that she would be working on Sundays. She had assumed that would be the domain of the minister and the organist. Her former job at the insurance office was strictly Monday through Friday, eight until five. Her weekends were her own. She knew that she dared not say any of that to Myrtle Hodges. Myrtle was a woman of formidability and common sense. If Julia had thought more about the actual job before she came to Pineville looking for some help for herself and some answers from her brother, she probably would have figured it out.

"Mondays are catch-up days from the weekend. There will be more mail on Monday, as well as all of the notes, requests, and other paperwork from any events or services over the weekend."

Reverend Plain peeked his head into the office. "How are you two ladies getting on?" he asked.

"Just fine, Reverend," Myrtle answered. "All in hand."

"I had no doubts," he said with a smile as he left to go back to his own office at the far side of the sanctuary.

"Now," Myrtle said, "Tuesdays are meeting days. We alternate who gets the church hall for those. This week is the Usher's Meeting. We don't need to be at that, or for most committee meetings for that matter. Most of them have their own people who keep track of things. They will leave notes on your desk to be typed, assigned, or processed."

Julia nodded her head in understanding.

"However, once a month, we have Church Council meetings. They start at seven o'clock, and we must attend. We keep the notes for all council meetings, and they must be meticulously recorded. The council handles all business for the church administration."

"I will be there," Julia said.

Myrtle said, "I think you've got the gist of it. You will come to find a schedule that works well for yourself. Get the work done. Be where you are supposed to be and take the rest of the time to try to figure out where you fit in town."

"I'm afraid that part I don't understand," Julia said.

"This is a very small town, Miss Garver. Each person finds where they fit. I was lucky to find this job after my husband passed thirty years ago. I was not a whole lot older than you then. I didn't have a clue how to be a thirty-four-year-old widow who had to somehow earn her own living with a high school education and few appreciable skills. I didn't know much in the way of being a secretary. Other than strong and determined, I didn't know which end was up. I just figured it out as I went along."

Myrtle looked Julia as straight in the face as anyone ever had. "What I did know is that I loved the small-town life. I had beautiful memories of my Arthur and I walking along Main Street, of boating on the river. Those memories are tied to this town, Miss Garver. I found fun in church bake sales and camaraderie at the library book club."

She took a deep breath before continuing. "You have secretarial skills. You've done this type of job before. That is a plus and will help you figure out how to get the church work done."

"Thank you," Julia said.

"What you will also need to figure out is how you, as a twenty-five-year-old young woman who is raising her sixteen-year-old brother, will thrive beyond that. Pineville is small, Miss Garver. Social opportunities don't have hundreds of outlets on a Saturday night. You are from a large city. Will you be able to live with that level of simplicity? We don't have major sports teams or summer festivals that bring in big celebrities to perform. Our sports come from the high school athletes. Our summer festivals have Donny Anderson playing the accordion or some of the other locals bringing out whatever talents they have. It's not for everyone."

Julia never considered all of that. "I'm looking forward to a more peaceful way of life for my brother and myself. I don't exactly know where or how that will happen yet, but I like it here so far."

"Fair enough," Myrtle said. "I hope you do find what you are seeking. Just start with what you know you need to do and move on from there."

Myrtle took Julia over to the copier to work on some of the requests from the Property Committee. The unit was smaller, older, and simpler than the one in her old office. "Questions?" Myrtle asked.

As they were collating and stapling the Property Committee packets, Myrtle continued to tell Julia about her time with Pineville Community Church. "This office wasn't even built back then. I worked wherever I found space. The administrative part of the church was a mess, no organization or procedures whatsoever," she said with a shake of her head and a click of her tongue.

"The reverend at that time was a bit of a scatterbrain. That man couldn't find a hammer if it were next to the nail. That is not the appropriate way to function in a place where people spend some of the most crucial moments of their lives."

Julia thought perhaps Myrtle Hodges was slightly overstating the importance of the order of things.

Myrtle continued, "They're baptized. They're confirmed. They're counseled. They get married. When life comes full circle, they have their funerals here."

Julia thought she head the older woman's voice break. A few hours ago, Julia wouldn't have thought that were even possible. "I can see you've done a lot for everyone here. I know I am not you, and I know you will be missed."

"This place is very dear to me," said Myrtle, "and to the people in this town. I know for some folks they would not consider this position to be career-building. Some people might think being a church secretary is just secretarial, Monday through Friday, eight until five."

Julia gulped and wondered if Myrtle Hodges read minds as a sideline.

"Being here will bring you days when you will thank God you were here to help someone, and it will bring you days when you will thank God it wasn't you that needed the kind of help that person needed."

Myrtle Hodges was a wise woman.

Chapter Six

At the end of the road where the street met the woods, just a couple of blocks away from the church and the parsonage where he was now living, sat Jeremy's new school. He discovered the previous night that he could see the football field from his bedroom window at the upstairs front of the house.

What he didn't realize at the time was that Pineville Area High School sat on the same plot of land as the middle school and the grade school. The buildings and the classes were relatively small and joining the buildings onto one property made sense for sharing things like support staff, gymnasium, sports, music and art rooms, plus a small theater.

It seemed odd to him to have kids from five-to-eighteen all heading to the same place. "Weird," he said to himself.

He stopped at the office, collected his locker number and schedule, and declined offers for a tour of the school or assistance in finding his classrooms. "My old school was five times this size," Jeremy said. "I think I can find them on my own."

"Your call," said the woman behind the counter.

Jeremy headed for the office door.

"Good luck here," she said.

"Yeah, whatever."

He headed off for his first class, Junior English, Room 103. As he thought, he found the classroom with no trouble. His English teacher introduced herself, gave him a textbook, and went on teaching. "Find a seat and jump in whenever you are ready." He found a seat in the back corner of the room where he could surreptitiously use his cell phone to text his Milwaukee friends.

"First period at Nowhere High. English. This woman thinks Shakespeare is interesting. Not even close. I think you have to live in some sort of alternate universe to be an English teacher."

Second period's only challenge was realizing that the gym was between the grade school and the middle school. It required a little longer walk to get there. The teacher wasn't thrilled Jeremy was a few minutes late but told him he was glad he now knew how to find the place. This unit taught archery. Members of the local archery club were on hand to help the gym teacher. Jeremy had never handled a bow and arrow before. It was not his natural gift. Then again, he was about as good at it as half the class. He didn't stand out too much.

On to third period, U.S. Government, Room 205. He made it back to the high school building on time and slid into another rear seat.

The cell phone came out again. *"Hey, actually even beat the teacher into this class. Maybe the guy won't even know I'm here. At least we won't be expected to read Shakespeare in this one."*

Jeremy saw a man standing right next to him.

"You can put the phone away, or you can give it to me. Cell phones are not allowed during class." The man needed no introduction. By his tone, Jeremy knew he was the U.S. Government teacher, and one that thought he could control everybody in it.

"Fine." He slid the phone into his shirt pocket.

The teacher did not move.

"I put it away. What more do you want?"

Lucas saw Jeremy's face. The snotty kid from the diner, and he was the new student in his class. "My name in Mr. Anderson. Apparently, you are Jeremy Garver."

"Yeah, that's me."

"Well, Jeremy. Since you seem to think that this is a place where people can do as they please, I will take a couple of minutes to introduce you to the rules of this room."

Even though Jeremy found Mr. Anderson somewhat intimidating, he refused to show it. He put the most bored look he could muster on his face and stared at him.

"First, in this room, everyone is valued, and we each have rights and responsibilities. Your rights are to be as cocky as you please and learn as little as you please. Your responsibilities are to treat everyone with respect and not to disrupt anyone else's opportunity to get what they want out of this class." The teacher continued, "My right is to be treated with respect, and my responsibility is to give you the best learning environment I am capable of giving all of my students. Are we clear on that?"

Jeremy put a second's worth of space between each punctuated word. "Yeah. Cocky. Learning. Clear."

Mr. Anderson didn't bat an eyelid or raise his voice. "I do not accept late work. You get it in on time, or it doesn't come across my desk at all."

"Fine."

"Here is your book and your syllabus. All the assignments, and their requirements, are listed on here. There's also a list of websites and reference books which could prove to be useful to you. Additionally, my office hours are listed should you want to come in for extra assistance. I offer that on the assumption that people have actually tried to do the work themselves first."

At lunch, Jeremy texted his friends again. *"Government teacher is a dictator!"*

Chapter Seven

Julia's afternoon was quiet. Myrtle had left at noon for her errands, and Deke had long ago finished repairing the step. The reverend had been working in his own office. Julia used this time to go over what Myrtle had told her in the morning and to make herself feel comfortable in her new job.

The ringing of the office phone prompted her attention. "Pineville Community Church, Julia Garver speaking."

"Miss Garver, this is the school secretary calling. One of your brother's teachers would like to meet with you after school today to discuss ways of helping him succeed in his new school."

"Oh, certainly," Julia said. She repeated what the school secretary told her. "4:15, Room 205, main door, Lucas Anderson. Got it. Thank you." She hung up the phone and tore the notes from the message pad.

"Another Anderson!" She shook her head, wondering whether she would ever meet all of the Andersons that lived in Pineville.

Julia knocked on her uncle's office door. "Got a minute?" she asked.

"Of course, Julia," he said. "Everything ok?"

"Well, I think so, but I want to ask you about a couple of things."

She walked into his office, which was only slightly larger than her own. The reverend's desk had the same beautiful sturdy wood as she was finding in other parts of the church. Bookshelves filled with religious, parenting, marriage, and counseling books took up the wall behind the desk. A small cross hung between the two narrow windows on the side wall.

There was such a feeling of comfort here. She felt that anyone entering this room would know the man behind the big wood desk was one of trust and compassion. Uncle Wilbur carried the weight of his position with the same measured, calm demeanor she observed whenever she was with him.

She sat in one of the two upholstered chairs that were opposite him. "What do you know about Lucas Anderson?"

"Lucas is one of Jeannie and Don's boys, the middle one, about," he paused to think, "hmm, about twenty-nine now, I would guess. He never left Pineville except when he went to college. He teaches all of the history and social studies at the high school."

"Is he a nice person, Uncle Wilbur?"

"Lucas Anderson is a good person, Julia, and a mighty fine teacher. If you go to Pineville Area High School, you get Lucas Anderson for at least a couple of those years."

"He wants to meet with me this afternoon to discuss how Jeremy can best succeed at school. That's good, isn't it?" Julia bit her lip.

The minister took another moment to collect his thoughts. "Yes, it is good, Julia. As I said, he's a wonderful teacher. He's innovative in his teaching style, and he cares very much about his students. If Lucas Anderson tells you something, it is something he holds true. He's direct, and he will help if he can."

"I'm so glad to hear that. Thank you. The meeting's at 4:15. So, I won't need to leave here until four o'clock." Julia took a slight gasp. "Oh, my gosh. I should have asked you first if that was all right. I'm sorry. I just, well, it was the school, and..."

Her uncle put up his hand to stop her. "It's fine, Julia. We all work together here. You do what you need to do. There will most likely be times when you will leave here late. It all works out."

Julia stopped just as she was about to exit his office. "Uncle Wilbur," she said, "just how many Andersons are there in Pineville?"

The minister laughed.

Shortly after four o'clock, Julia gathered her things and headed out the church door to the high school. The short walk gave her some time to think about the upcoming meeting with Jeremy's teacher. She reflected on her earlier conversation with her uncle. He had said Lucas Anderson was a good man, wonderful teacher, and would help if he could. Julia felt herself relax and smile. She could picture a kind, quiet man who could give Jeremy the caring support and sympathetic guidance he so desperately needed. She wondered if he would be quiet like his father, Don Anderson, or funny like his uncle, Deke. She was eager to meet her next Mr. Anderson.

Chapter Eight

Lucas was seated at his desk grading papers when Julia entered the room. She noticed his dark hair and broad shoulders, how the muscles in his upper arms strained slightly against the fabric of his pale gray sweater.

"Mr. Anderson?" she asked.

"Yes, come in, Miss Garver," he said as he raised his head from looking at the papers.

When their eyes met, each recognized the other from the previous day's encounter at the Pineville Diner. Both pairs of eyes steeled their gazes.

His tone changed. It matched the look in those dark brown eyes. "Have a seat." He pointed to one of the student desks at the front and center of the classroom.

Julia's lips tightened and pressed together before she replied, "Of course." Slender as she was, she had to turn herself sideways to fit into the cramped space. She was about to say something to him about his behavior yesterday at the diner, but she remembered she was there for Jeremy. "I understand you think you may be able to help my brother do better at the school. I appreciate that."

"I said I wanted to *try* to help your brother, Miss Garver. There is a big difference, and the difference is him."

Julia sat up as straight as she could in the confining student chair. "What exactly do you mean by that, Mr. Anderson?"

Lucas wondered if the attractive blonde woman sitting across from him was immune to the boy's attitude or daft as a post. He opted for leading with his first instinct. "Surely you've noticed that your brother has a bit of an attitude problem."

"Jeremy can be abrupt at times, but he has gone through a lot in sixteen years. If you read his file, you might have noticed that we have lost both our parents, and recently, our grandmother. That takes a toll, Mr. Anderson."

He sighed. "I did read his file, front to back, and I am aware of his losses in life. I agree that is difficult and requires a level of care, compassion, and thorough understanding of your brother's life that I do not possess."

"Thank you."

"Nonetheless," Lucas continued, "to call your brother 'a little abrupt' is to me, a gross understatement. He is disrespectful and feels entitled. He seems to want everyone to bow to his snarky behavior and to give into him. I will do neither."

Julia's tone became a bit agitated. "Thank you for clarifying your position. I will check in with the office in the morning to arrange for Jeremy to be moved to a classroom with a teacher who actually cares about him."

Lucas gave a short, mirthless laugh. "Good luck with that, Miss Garver. I am the only teacher at this school who teaches U.S. Government, and it's a required course."

"How could my uncle say you were a good person and teacher? I find you cold and heartless. You don't even care that a sixteen-year-old boy has had three significant losses in his life, one only a few months ago."

"I never said I didn't care about those things, Miss Garver. I assure you, I do. I know that tragedies such as these can leave scars and take time to process."

Julia looked up at the clock above Lucas's head and then back at him. "Something doesn't add up here," she said. "One minute you're telling me that my brother is a disrespectful spoiled brat, and the next minute you say you understand what he is going through in his life. Which is it?"

"Both." He looked deeper into her blue eyes. She looked perplexed to him.

He wondered if he was being unclear. No one ever accused him of being unclear before. He was known for stating how he felt and explaining point blank why he believed the way he did. Few people ever left a conversation with Lucas Anderson not fully and clearly understanding his position on any matter.

He tried again. "What I read in your brother's file is that he is a very bright student who has gone through more than any kid his age should. He has had a lot of emotional upheaval, and that will take a lot of work, time, and perhaps some counseling to help him get back to solid emotional ground."

"Yes," Julia answered. "I agree."

"However, he is also hurting himself even more right now with his attitude. The way he acts will push away the very people he encounters who could help him the most. One of my concerns is that if he continues with this present behavior and attitude, he will find himself with a circle of so-called friends who are also struggling with self-sabotaging behaviors."

"That is one of the reasons we moved here. Jeremy has made some questionable choices in friends lately," Julia said. "They're not bad kids," she hurried to add, "but I think they are pushing too many limits in too many ways. Hopefully, they will outgrow that as I am hoping my brother will."

"There's more," said Lucas. "If he continues to behave this way, he will fall behind in his studies, and not pull the grades that he is quite capable of getting. He is a little over a year away from college, should he wish to do that, and just about at the point where looking and applying for universities is generally advised. So, unfortunately, now is the worst time to let his grades and study habits slide."

"And you have a plan to fix all of this?" Julia asked.

"Not all of it," Lucas answered. "I am not a counselor. I can only give you the contact information of the one here at the school to get the best guidance on those very real, and important, concerns. I've put her card in the packet I've prepared for you, along with all of the other contact numbers for the school, club opportunities, and so forth that we have here."

"Jeremy may feel a counselor is not necessary, but I will talk to him."

"There is also information about other professional, government, and community services and opportunities offered in the Pineville area in the packet. Many things are in surrounding towns, but we aren't all that far away from almost anything you may need."

She eyed the size of the packet one more time. "I'm not sure exactly where to start with all of this. Jeremy might not want to look at any of it."

Lucas's eyes went to steel one more time. "Who is the guardian here, Miss Garver, your brother or you?" The moment the words were out of his mouth, he regretted saying them.

He was a good teacher and was always viewed as being fair-minded and concerned for his students and their families. Those were some of his strong points.

The other side was that he did not tolerate indecision well. He was a person who analyzed facts, made a plan, and with rare exception, stuck to it. People didn't have to agree with Lucas Anderson. They just needed to analyze their own facts, make their own plan and then move forward.

All the progress that had been made in the last few minutes seemed to be gone again. Julia's anger was peaking as she thought over some of the teacher's comments.

"Look, Mr. Anderson," Julia said, "the changes in both my brother's and my lives over the past couple of months have been difficult. While I do not expect you to understand all of those changes, I do expect you to understand that there have been many, many decisions to make and to understand that I may need some time and thought to make even more."

"Of course," said Lucas. "I apologize. My concern, as Jeremy's teacher, is only that you do consider what is best for him, then proceed accordingly. It is my hope that this information will help you with any resources, school or community, that you may need to begin that process."

Julia tried to find a comfortable position in the uncomfortable seat. "Is there anything else?"

"Yes, and that is the main reason why I asked to see you."

"What would that be?"

"This class. I've already spoken directly to Jeremy regarding the behavioral expectations I have."

"It is your classroom, Mr. Anderson. Assuming your guidelines are realistic, Jeremy will be told he is to follow them."

"Good," said Lucas, "and, now, for his academics."

Judging from the quarter-inch thick pack of sheets he had in his hands, Julia felt this part of the conference would be as arduous as the first.

Lucas said, "Jeremy has quite a bit of catching up to do since he had not yet taken this course at his former school. As far as all the textbook readings go, I really think your brother will have no difficulty comprehending the facts and figures. It may take some extra reading time, but he is bright, and some of this material was actually covered in his U.S. History class from his Milwaukee high school."

"That sounds good. Jeremy is a good reader, and up until quite recently, his grades were strong as well."

"However, as you know, we are only a couple weeks away from spring break. After which, this class will head into its main project of the year. In this particular class, we do a Government in Action project in lieu of a final exam. I find that when the students do this type of work, they come away with a far better understanding of our governmental system versus just memorizing the facts. It's putting those facts, and the interplay of those facts, into action. Many of my students find this a fun and engaging project."

"I hope Jeremy feels the same way." Julia knew that her brother found little in which to engage himself these days other than his phone.

"I hope so, too, Miss Garver," Lucas said. "This project will amount to fifty percent of his grade."

"I will let him know that."

"One other thing about the Government in Action project," he said.

"Yes?"

"It's a group project. He will be paired with other students. Together, they will more fully delve into the same particular branch of the government and do a thorough examination on that branch. His performance with this project will impact not only his own grade, but that of the other students in that group."

"I will definitely tell him that and encourage him to do his best."

"Please do. I put a few names on a list of people to whom he can reach out for questions or to form a study group. He can also always come to me, of course."

"Ok, thank you."

"However, I know students often find it more enjoyable to work with other students rather than their teacher."

Julia reflected on how demanding and terse Lucas Anderson could be. "I can understand that."

"At first, I thought of pairing him with a couple of boys from the class. Unfortunately, I don't think any of them would be the right matches for him. They will either get irritated with his current attitude, or worse yet, they will just give up and slack off with him. Neither one of those is productive. So, I have given him the names of two of the girls in the class who have offered to work with him. The first one is Robin Lee who is one of the most upbeat, positive girls in the school. She will be an excellent source of making the time enjoyable. The second one is my sister, Angela. She needed some coaxing from me on this, but she is tough as nails and won't let him slack."

"That must be a family characteristic," Julia found herself saying aloud.

She took the packet with all of the information and slid it into her tote bag. "Is there anything else?" she asked.

"Two more things I will suggest to you as things that could assist Jeremy in finding a good circle of friends in a shorter time period."

"And those would be?"

"Joining a club, sport or a group of some sort will help him find people who are interested in some of the same things he is. Most of the clubs have been going since the beginning of the school year, so at this late date, you might want to hold off until fall for those. However, the spring musical is coming up, and the spring sport season is just getting underway. With one of those, he could get involved at the same time as the other students. He would not be the only new person out there."

"You mentioned there were two things. What would the second one be?" Julia asked.

"Assuming his grades stay strong, as I am relatively certain they can, encourage him to find a part-time job. Not only would that introduce him to more people, but it would give him some spending money that he earned himself. There's a sense of pride in that."

Julia didn't think her brother was job-ready at this time, but she remembered how much she had enjoyed her first job at the ice cream shop. "Once he is settled in here, I will talk to him about that, too."

"Miss Garver," Lucas said, "I know you think I am giving you a lot of advice right now, virtually all of it non-requested. You may well feel that it is too much at once. It might be. However, don't sell that job idea short. Not only will it do all of those things I already mentioned, but there are a couple more areas in which that could prove beneficial."

"Oh?"

"It will teach him more about boundaries and responsibility. It will also give him someone other than you to whom he is accountable. Not to be insulting, Miss Garver, but I saw the two of you at the diner yesterday, and you allow that boy to walk all over you."

Chapter Nine

When Julia stepped into the kitchen, she found Jeremy eating a bowl of cereal. "Thanks for dinner," he said.

The conversation with Lucas Anderson had been challenging enough. She was not ready for another difficult one with her brother this soon. "Why didn't you heat up some leftovers from last night while you waited?"

"How?" Jeremy asked. "This kitchen is so out-of-date. It doesn't even have a microwave."

"You can use the oven, Jeremy. Just don't put any plastic dishes in there."

"I'm not stupid, Julia," he said. "Where were you anyway? I thought you would be home before now."

This was not the way Julia wanted to bring up the conversation she had with his history teacher. She really wanted to talk to her uncle first. "I'm surprised Uncle Wilbur isn't home by now."

"He was. Some woman named Myrtle called, and he left again. Said he had to go see some guy in the hospital. Had some kind of fall or something."

Julia remembered Myrtle telling her about some of the non-business-hour activities for both the minister and the secretary.

"I hope whomever fell is all right," she said.

Jeremy shrugged. "He didn't say. All I know is that woman called, and he left. He did say he might be late getting back and not to hold dinner for him."

He held up the empty cereal bowl. "Any chance that dinner is going to happen anytime soon? I promised my friends that I would do video games online with them tonight."

As she retrieved the leftovers from the refrigerator and started the oven, she said, "No video games tonight."

"What?"

"You started a new school that's three-fourths of the way through the school year. I am positive you have a lot of areas where you need to get caught up."

"It's no big deal."

"Yes, it is, Jeremy. I don't know where Pineville High is with math and English and such compared to Milwaukee, but I do know that U.S. Government is a new course for you. You will need to do a lot of reading to get to where the other students are."

"That teacher told me he didn't care how much I learned in that class."

Color crept up Julia's cheeks. She wondered whether it was Lucas Anderson or Jeremy who was lying to her. "That's not the impression I got from him."

Jeremy slammed the now empty cereal bowl on the table and looked at her. "You went to see my teachers? I'm a junior in high school!"

"I went to see your government teacher. The school called me, and it was he who requested the meeting."

"That's ridiculous! He thinks everybody should do everything his way. He's some sort of control freak. One text message to my friends, and he calls my big sister. What a joke."

"This is anything but a joke, Jeremy," Julia said. "There is a huge project due at the end of the year, and it's a group thing. Not only does your grade in that class depend on how you do, but so do others'."

"I don't care."

"Well, you used to care, and you have to care. We start looking at colleges in the summer and tanking your grades won't give you many options. Letting a group of other kids down won't give you many options for friends, either."

"Those kids weren't exactly lining up to get to know me today. I couldn't tell you one single name."

Julia immediately softened. The thought of her brother in this new environment without any friends whatsoever was another thing that never occurred to her. In her rush to get him away from the questionable friends he was starting to make in Milwaukee, she neglected to think about the lack of friends he would initially have in Pineville.

There were so many things she hadn't completely weighed before making this move. The hours on the job, whether or not she or her brother would fit into small-town life, her brother's lack of friends or support out here, so many considerations. Plus, these were the things that had been brought to her attention on just her first full-day there. She again felt that she was failing her brother, and that was one thing Julia would not allow herself to do.

Maybe Lucas Anderson was right about some things, she thought. "Jeremy," Julia began, "Mr. Anderson has some suggestions for helping you get to know people quicker out here and a few other things."

The flatness of her brother's tone left her no doubt that he didn't put much faith in how appealing he would find his teacher's suggestions to be. "Really."

"Yes," Julia said. She tried to counterbalance her brother's disregard by starting with the most positive things. "He said you were bright and should have no problem catching up in class, that he has a couple of girls who offered to be in a study group with you on that big project."

"Swell."

"He also thought it would be great if you would try out for one of the spring sports."

"Don't think so."

The constant negativity from her brother, in conjunction with the busy and rough day she had, was wearing her down. "What about trying out for the spring musical?"

"Nope." With that, Jeremy left the kitchen and headed to his room.

Julia sat at the kitchen table with her head in her hands. The tears were starting to flow, and she found herself unable to stop them. She could not fall apart. She had to stay strong for her brother. The decision to move to Pineville had been hers, and now it was up to her to find a way to make this work if there was any way to at all to do so.

She put the food in the oven, though she wasn't sure if it would get eaten, fished her phone out of her purse, and called the one person whom she felt would be sympathetic and agree with her.

"Hi, Stephanie," she said.

"You sound like you're crying. What happened?"

After a few more moments of tears, Julia began telling her best friend about her not-so-best day. "I should have never told Jeremy what that man said without talking to Uncle Wilbur first."

"What man? What did he say? Why are you this upset?"

"Jeremy's U.S. Government teacher, Lucas Anderson, he wanted a conference to 'help him adjust faster' at the new school."

"That's a bad thing? What were his suggestions, and why are you crying??"

"I should have known not to trust him as soon as I saw that he was the same jerk that gave us that nasty look in the diner yesterday."

"Wait? The guy that looks like a movie star?"

"I never said he looked like a movie star. I said he was good-looking enough to find someone to put up with his garbage."

Julia stopped crying and some irritation rose in her voice. She never had this reaction before. "Stephanie, I tried to talk to Jeremy about his suggestions just now."

"I take it that didn't go so well."

"No."

Stephanie knew Julia. For her to be this upset, there had to be more to the discussions. "You still haven't told me what his suggestions were. Maybe he's actually trying to help."

"He told me Jeremy is disrespectful and doesn't want to try."

"Jules, you told me yourself that Jeremy's attitude was getting worse over the last few months. He's bound to be struggling with Margaret's death and maybe that brought up some unresolved issues from your folks."

"On that we all agree," said Julia.

Stephanie said, "Plus, our Bro-Bro is a teenager. They come built in with all sorts of angst and adjustment issues. Surely, your teacher-friend understands that."

Julia sighed. "He is no friend of mine. He's arrogant, and he things he has every answer. Tell me, Stephanie, what do you think of the idea of Jeremy try a spring sport?"

"It will help him make friends faster and get a new comfort zone."

"Hmmm."

"Hmmm, what?" asked Stephanie.

"That's what Lucas Anderson said," said Julia.

"So at least he has one decent suggestion."

"He has two of the girls from the class helping Jeremy with a study group for the final class project."

"And you don't like that? Why?" asked Stephanie.

"I do like it," said Julia, "but I'm afraid that Jeremy will not make much effort and let those other kids down."

"How is that Lucas Anderson's fault? Not that I'm siding with him or anything. I just want to know why you are so upset with this guy."

Julia said, "He put together this big packet of information for me with just about every phone number and email address in the whole doggone town. There are numbers in there for the club advisors, the sports coaches, the school counselor, the park district, the library, the local dentist, and just about anything else you could name. I don't think there's much he didn't include."

"It sounds to me as though this guy is looking out for him."

"And he said I let Jeremy walk all over me."

"So, he's a touch abrupt."

"A touch abrupt? Stephanie, that man is incorrigible!"

"I just figured out the problem. It's sooooo obvious," Stephanie said.

"What's that?" asked Julia.

"He's hitting all your nerves at the same time."

"Huh?"

"He knows you are worried about your brother. He senses you feel you are in over your head, whether or not that is actually the case – and you find him attractive."

Julia could not believe what her friend was saying. "Seriously? I've told you that man thinks he has all the answers."

"And you my dear friend, often feel like you have none of them. Maybe between the two of you, you will find a few things that will actually help all of this."

"There is no 'two of us', Stephanie."

"Yes, whether you think so or not, there is. He's your brother's teacher, who has reached out to help however he can. You are your brother's guardian, who wants to help him more than anything."

"Ok, so as a guardian-teacher thing, yes. However, I don't know if Jeremy will take any of those suggestions. I don't sense that's going to go exceptionally well."

"You're conveniently neglecting the other part of this, my BFF. You are most definitely attracted to this guy. That tone in your voice hasn't been used since Davy Marlowe told you that you were the prettiest girl in the school."

"That was eighth grade."

"Need I say more?"

"Stephanie, I have zero time for attractions, and I am not looking for one."

"That's the thing about attractions, Julia. They don't wear the same watch we do. They don't care about our calendars or our commitments. They come up out of nowhere, often when we least expect them or even want them."

Julia chuckled. "That's kind of funny."

"What do you mean?"

"Jeremy calls Pineville, 'Nowhere'. Now you just said attractions come up out of 'nowhere'."

"I miss you, Jules, but I think 'Nowhere' is precisely where you need to be."

Chapter Ten

"Heading to the dictator's class. Somebody ought to tell this guy that we are a democracy, not a regime." Jeremy finished his text right as he walked in the classroom door. Seeing Lucas Anderson, he made a display of showing him he was sliding the phone into his pocket.

He took the same seat at the back of the class. Feigning boredom, and with his eyes closed, Jeremy actually listened to the discussion on last night's assignment. He had read the chapter the night before. This unit covered some of the tumult of the sixties and how this would impact some of the forthcoming laws and decisions in the United States.

At the end of the class, Jeremy heard someone rather loudly clear his or her throat. He slowly opened his eyes, expecting to give whomever it was a pointed look to leave him alone. He was surprised to see two girls standing next to his desk.

The Asian girl had a sweet smile and extended her hand to shake his. "Hi, Jeremy," she said. "I'm Robin, one of the people who want to be in a study group with you. We're going to get a little head start on the Government in Action project. We'd love for you to start with us."

The little blonde looked downright hostile. She handed him a piece of paper. "We're meeting twice a week out at the Pineville Diner after school, Tuesday and Fridays."

"I don't drive yet," Jeremy said.

"That's ok," Robin said, "I do, and we'll all drive out there together."

"Well, see, here's the thing," said Jeremy. "I usually eat dinner after school."

"It's a diner," the blonde replied.

"Well, I'm not sure we can afford for me to eat out twice a week," said Jeremy.

The little blonde didn't look as though she wanted to be a part of anything involving Jeremy. "It's my parents' place. Just show up. They'll feed you."

Sarcasm was one of Jeremy's specialties. He looked straight into the blonde girl's eyes. "Well, since you're so friendly and all, I'll be there," he said.

Robin said, "Great! Meet you at the office after school. See you at four o'clock!"

The bell rang signaling the end of the class. The girls headed for the door before Jeremy could grab his books and get out of the desk seat.

"Wait," said Jeremy. "You mean tonight??"

To Julia's surprise, she saw a text from her brother at lunchtime.

"Going to study group out at that diner. Have a ride."

Julia allowed herself a small smile. "Whether it's making new friends or getting his grades back, I sure hope this somehow works."

Chapter Eleven

Myrtle's calendar told Julia that Wednesday afternoon would be spent setting up the fellowship hall for the Lenten Supper that evening. The older woman had said that she would be at the church that afternoon to show Julia how the set-up worked.

Once the volunteers arrived, Myrtle went into her leadership mode, giving each person tasks and checking each item off her list. Tables were moved a little, here or there, so each seat had ample space to get in and out. Chairs were straightened. Food that had already arrived was organized into types. Slow cookers were plugged into outlets. Salads went to the fridge. Three large industrial-size coffee pots were brought out of the back and set onto the beverage station, along with the basket of assorted tea bags, creamer pitchers and sugar bowls. Desserts went to a side table festooned with a fresh white tablecloth and some fresh flowers, which someone had brought with them. The small team began setting the tables with water pitchers, placemats, napkins, silverware, coffee cups, and water glasses.

The only volunteer Julia already knew was Deke, but by the end of the set-up, she had mastered the names of all six of the others. She even knew that Glynnis Oaks served on the church council, ran the local beauty shop, and thought that 'a few highlights would really bring out the blue in Julia's eyes'.

In between assignments and tasks, Myrtle showed Julia every step she was taking. Julia wondered whether the volunteers really needed Myrtle to get this done, or whether they just knew that Myrtle would tell them what to do anyway. Either way, the system worked.

"As all of you know," Myrtle announced to her team, "next week is one of our busiest weeks of the year. We have one Maundy Thursday service, two Good Friday services, and a prayer vigil on Saturday. Easter Sunday has Sunrise Service at six, pancake breakfast at eight, Easter egg hunt for the children at nine, and final service at ten. Plus, Saturday afternoon, the high schoolers come and set out the eggs for the hunt. Additionally, the pancake breakfast volunteers come and get this room ready for the breakfast. Of course, the Easter breakfast will have three times as many people as we will have with us tonight. I know some of you already volunteered to help with the breakfast, but please spread the word to your friends and family. More help is always appreciated."

The potluck supper was set to begin at six in the evening. By five-thirty, the coffee was percolating, and the food was being set on serving tables. Congregants began to trickle in to the hall. Reverend Plain had joined Julia and Myrtle downstairs and stood at the entry door greeting those as they arrived.

Julia was starting to relax. Although it had been a long day with both her office work and setting up the hall, she found herself happy in the tasks and getting to know some of the other church members.

"Good evening, folks," the minister called out above the crowd's chatter. "It looks like we're about ready to start dinner."

Sounds of agreement filtered through the hall.

He continued, "I want to thank you all for bringing this wonderful food tonight. It is always a pleasure to have a meal together and to visit with so many of you. After we have our prayer, you are welcome to get in line and help yourselves."

Julia and the other volunteers stopped their work to bow their heads with the rest of the group.

"Dear Lord," Reverend Plain began. "We thank you for this delicious food, for all of the volunteers, and for our time together. We thank you for every person here at Pineville Community Church, the established members and the new ones. May we grow in your love and fellowship. Amen."

Julia busied herself in the church kitchen with a few others making certain the food in the buffet line stayed restocked, and any empty dishes were placed in the kitchen to be washed and dried. She waited with the reverend, Myrtle, and the other volunteers until the line dwindled before going for her own food. She had skipped lunch, and many of the pots and platters of hot dishes, side dishes, cookies, pies, and cakes looked tempting.

"Julia!" a cheerful voice called. "Come sit with us!"

Julia turned to see Jeannie, the friendly waitress and co-owner of the Pineville Diner calling to her. She smiled as she walked toward Jeannie. The rest of these folks had to be more of the family, Julia mused. She saw Deke and Don, followed by a teenage girl, a man in a sheriff's uniform, two small children, and Lucas. She stopped short. "Hi, Jeannie," she said. "That's really quite nice of you, but-"

"Mother, our table's already full," Lucas said.

Jeannie sent a questioning look toward her second-oldest son. "Where are your manners, Lucas?" We can scooch in a bit to make room for a new neighbor."

"Really," Julia said, "I don't want to make you folks uncomfortable."

"Nonsense," said Jeannie. "Get another chair, Lucas, and we'll just slide over a little."

Lucas looked as though he was about to say more, but his mother stood next to Julia with her hands on her hips indicating she did not want to discuss the matter any further. Behind his mother and Julia stood a glowering Myrtle.

Lucas went over to an empty table at the back of the room. He brought a chair back to the family table. He discovered the one opening his family had created was right between himself and his five-year-old niece. He slid the empty chair in the spot.

"Miss Garver, won't you please sit down?" Lucas asked.

"Thank you," Julia replied as she sat, "and you can call me Julia if you want."

The teenager at the table said, "Oh, you must be Jeremy's sister. I'm Angela. Thanks to my brother, Jeremy is on the same government project team as my friend, Robin and I."

Julia wasn't quite sure how happy Angela was to be in that little group, but she decided to stay positive and upbeat if possible. After all, Jeannie extended kindness to her twice in the short period of time she had been in this town. "Yes, your brother told me about that. I'm so happy you are willing to help him."

"I'm not helping him."

Julia thought that sounded as though it could have come straight from Lucas Anderson's mouth. "Well, um, thanks for including him."

"Robin and I do a lot of things together, and anyone who does a project with us knows that we work hard," Angela said. "I think Jeremy found that out last night."

"How did he do?" asked Julia.

"He's not stupid," said Angela.

"Angela Renee!" Jeannie chastised.

Jeannie directed her focus at Julia. "I'm sorry, Julia," she said. "You must think my family has no manners at all. I apologize."

"No," said Julia. "I understand it can be very hard to adjust to new people."

"Well," said Deke, "you're sure getting to know a lot of new folks quickly, Julia. Some mighty strong ones at that."

Julia nodded.

Myrtle made an announcement over the crowd. "Five minutes until service! Please finish up and head on over to the sanctuary."

Deke continued, "If Myrtle hasn't run you off yet, you can probably handle us Andersons."

Julia heard the beginning hymn of the evening as she and two of the remaining volunteers stayed behind for clean-up and the dinner dishes. She was lost in thought and soap suds as she heard a voice next to her.

"I'm sorry if I offended you, Miss Garver," Lucas said. "It was not my intention."

"I'm fine," said Julia.

"And I'm sorry I said your brother wasn't stupid," said Angela, who was standing directly beside her brother. Hearing her own words, Angela let out a groan. "I mean, it's not that he's actually stupid or anything, because he's not. It's just," she shrugged.

"I knew what you meant," said Julia. "It's ok, Angela. I know it wasn't your idea to study with Jeremy. Your brother told me that. I want you to know that I appreciate that you are making the effort to include him and help him feel more comfortable here."

"He's actually kind of smart, you know," said Angela.

"Thank you. I hope he works as hard as you and your friend."

"I've got to go back to church now," said Angela. "My mom told me to apologize and come back in time for the sermon."

Lucas remained standing next to the sink when Angela left.

"Is there something else you want to say to me, Mr. Anderson?" Julia asked.

"Yes, a few things."

Julia went back to washing the dishes. "Go ahead," she said.

"Can you stop washing those dishes for a while so we can have a conversation?" he asked.

"It's been a long day, and I would like to get home before nine."

"Move over," he said.

"What?"

"Move over. I'll wash. You dry, and we'll both get home by nine."

Julia was happy for the extra help at the sink, but not so sure she wanted to hear what he wished to say.

"What did you want to tell me?" she asked.

"First of all, I do apologize if I sounded as though I didn't want you at the table. Frankly, I didn't think you would want to sit anywhere near me. I thought I would give you an easy way to leave without telling my mother that."

Julia hadn't considered that possibility.

"I also wanted to ask you how your brother is doing. I actually caught him with his eyes open in class today," said Lucas.

Julia gave him a questioning look.

"It's a first," Lucas said. "He likes to pretend he's asleep."

"I will talk to him about that," Julia said.

"No, don't," said Lucas. "If he thinks he's one up on me, that's fine."

"Look," said Julia, "I think we got off to a bad start. I can see already that a couple of your suggestions are helping him, even if he won't admit it yet."

"Glad to hear it." Lucas stopped washing the dishes.

Julia stopped drying mid-plate. "Is there something else?"

"Yes," Lucas said. "How are you?"

"Things at home are improving," she said.

"I'm not talking about your home, Julia. I'm not talking about your brother, your uncle, or your great-aunt's nephew's podiatrist. I want to know how you are."

Julia was not prepared for that; maybe from Stephanie, but definitely not from Lucas Anderson. "I'm fine."

"That's not much of an answer."

"I'm not really sure how to answer. I haven't been here long. I'm still adjusting."

"What's different here?" asked Lucas.

Julia let out a nervous chuckle. "Most things are different here. This job is different. I worked at an insurance company office back in Milwaukee. Came in at eight. Filed and typed all day. Went home at five."

"Did you like that?"

"Not really."

"Then why did you stay?"

"I got used to it," Julia said. "The people were decent to me when my grandmother was ill, and they understood why I wanted to move here."

"Why exactly was that?"

Julia felt herself stiffen. "I wanted Jeremy to be in a more nurturing environment with a new start."

Lucas would not lessen his gaze. "Are you saying the only reason you came to Pineville, Wisconsin, of all the possible places on planet Earth, was for your brother to have a new start, that this change had nothing at all to do with you?"

Julia put the plate in the cupboard and faced Lucas. "All right. Stop. You want me to confess? Well, I guess here in church would be one of the best possible places for that. Wouldn't it?" Julia's face was getting a bit pink, and her voice raised half an octave.

"Yes," she said, "it's for me, too. I'm twenty-five-years-old, and I am left to 'raise' my sixteen-year-old brother. You want the truth, Mr. Anderson?"

Lucas stayed silent.

"I don't have a clue as to how to do it. I know how to be a sister. I know how to be a friend. However, I have never been a parent before. I am fumbling and making a mess out of my brother's life. My parents were great parents. My grandmother was a great parent. Me? I'm trying, but I am not them. I'm just plain scared."

She picked up another dish to dry.

"You want to know why I chose Pineville? That one's easy," she continued. "My one and only remaining relative is here. He's my grandmother's brother, and he is, as you know, a minister. I thought he would be the best influence I could find for Jeremy, and maybe, just maybe, help me get a full-night's sleep instead of tossing around worrying what I was going to screw up next."

Lucas was surprised at the strength of her emotions. He wiped his hands on another dish towel and put his hand on Julia's shoulder. "I'm sorry, Julia," he said. "I really am. If I can help in any way," he began.

Julia threw down her dish towel. She wasn't sure how to handle Lucas's closeness. She eased away from his hand. "Just help Jeremy," she said.

Lucas's voice took on a more assertive tone. "What are you so afraid of?"

"I told you. I don't want to make things worse for my brother."

"There's more."

"I'm not one of your students, Mr. Anderson."

"Meaning what? That I am not allowed to talk to you outside of the high school or about anything other than your brother?"

"Of course not. I just... I'm... I'm fine."

"Julia, you can't even answer that question. Can you?"

"What exactly do you want me to say?"

"I'm guessing it was someone else who suggested you move here in the first place. I'm guessing it was someone else who suggested you work here at the church. Why do you feel you can't make your own decisions?"

Her eyes glared with indignation. "How dare you think you can know me for a couple of days and have everything so neatly figured out."

With that, soap still in the sink, and several dishes to go, Julia did something she had never done before. She turned on her heel and went straight out the door.

Chapter Twelve

Julia crossed the short path from the church to the parsonage as quickly as she could. In her haste to get away from Lucas and his probing, she had left without her coat. While not bitter cold this time of year, Wisconsin didn't get spring temperatures until well after Easter.

She entered through the back door into the kitchen. She made herself a cup of tea to warm the remaining chill.

Lucas Anderson was a perplexing and exasperating man. On the one hand, Julia was pleased that the suggestions he had made for Jeremy were working. On the other, she was angry with him for questioning her about herself. He made her feel weak, and Julia could not afford weakness. She had made the choice to move to Pineville, she thought.

She went further back in her memories. Grandma Margaret had brought Uncle Wilbur and Pineville up to her when she was ill. Then, however, it was only a conversation. No plans were made.

Julia sipped her tea. The warmth and quiet brought her reminiscences a little forward. At her grandmother's funeral,

Uncle Wilbur had told her he would always be there for her and Jeremy.

"Anytime, anything," her uncle had said, "just call. I will do whatever I can for both of you."

Julia didn't like where her thoughts were going. One more unbid memory came to her.

"Julia," Stephanie had said about a month ago, "you need to reach out to your uncle. You are doing your best, but our little Bro-Bro needs a firmer voice than yours."

When Julia tried to stop her, Stephanie continued. "You also need to start getting your own life moving forward. You've put it on hold for an awfully long time, and you are living your life being afraid of so much of what could be really good for you."

As much as Julia hated to admit it, the more she sat, and the more she thought through various chapters in her life, she realized that few of the decisions she felt she had made really began with her. The church secretary job had been her uncle's idea. Her filing job at the insurance company came to her through a former neighbor who already worked there. Even the job at the ice cream store had been because Stephanie wanted them both to apply together. None of those decisions were bad choices, but maybe they weren't the ones she would have picked for herself, she thought.

"No, that can't be me," Julia said aloud. "I may not demand my way like some people I've just met, but I am not a wishy-washy person."

She drained her tea cup. "I hate Lucas Anderson," she said.

She rinsed the cup in the sink and headed upstairs.

Julia paused at the entry to her brother's room. She had not seen him all day with having spent the better part of twelve hours at the church. She knocked on the door.

There was no answer.

"Jeremy," she said, "It's me. I want to talk to you." She turned the door knob and opened the door slightly.

"Jeremy? Are you asleep already?"

She opened the door all the way and found him gone.

Chapter Thirteen

Julia raced down the stairs and back to the church. Service had finished and most people had left. Since the lights were still lit, she ran inside the building through the front door. In doing so, she almost collided with her uncle and the Anderson family. "Um, I'm sorry," she blurted. "I don't mean to interrupt, but my brother is missing!" Her breath was coming in gasps from running and from worry.

"Oh, no," said Jeannie.

Joseph Anderson came and stood next to her. He was taller and brawnier than his brother and still in his sheriff's uniform from the day. "Let's have a seat in the church here, and then you can tell me exactly what happened."

Julia dutifully walked to the back pew in the sanctuary and took a seat.

Joseph already had a pad and pen in his hands to take notes. "When was the last time you saw him?" he asked.

"Um," Julia rubbed her hand over her forehead and bit her lip, "last night around ten when I was going up to bed."

"You didn't see him at all today?" asked the sheriff.

"No, he was still asleep, I think, when I came into work."

"He was in school," Lucas interjected. "At least he was there before lunch in my class."

"I saw him at the end of the day at his locker," Angela said.

"Ok," Joseph said. "That's good, Julia. That means he hasn't gotten as far."

"Oh," said Julia. "Good."

"Has anyone seen him since school let out?" the sheriff asked.

Although each person looked at the others, no one said they did.

"Was there a note of any kind at the house?" Joseph asked.

"Not that I saw," said Julia.

"Were any of his belongings missing? Clothes, money, personal things that might mean something to him?"

"I didn't really notice anything," said Julia. "I mean, I didn't look at everything. I just saw that he was gone."

"Did you talk to your brother at all today?" Joseph asked.

"No."

"Is that unusual?" he asked.

Julia caught her breath. "Not lately," she said. "We talk to each other about things, but not just to talk."

"How many messages have you left for him, Julia?" the sheriff asked.

"I haven't left any yet," Julia said.

"What?!" yelled Lucas. "You come running over here, upset as I've ever seen anyone, and you haven't even tried to contact him?!"

"I'm, I'm sorry," Julia said. "I didn't think to call him. I just saw that he wasn't home and panicked."

Joseph, and a few other Andersons, gave Lucas a cautionary look.

"Julia," Joseph said with a calm voice, "why don't you try to call him now? In the meantime, I will get a few arrangements made so that in the event he doesn't pick up or call you back, we can get moving on locating him."

"Ok, thank you," said Julia. "I need to go back to the house. I left my purse and phone there."

"How about if I come with you, Julia?" Jeannie asked. "We can make that call and do a bit of looking around the house to see if he left a note telling you where he was going."

"Thank you," said Julia.

"Mom," Joseph said.

"Yes?" said Jeannie.

"You might want to have her text him as well. Kids today don't always answer regular phone calls."

"We will do that, Joseph," Jeannie said.

"Mom," Lucas said.

"Yes, Lucas."

"You might want to also have her call that friend of hers from Milwaukee. Jeremy might have contacted her."

"Sounds good," Jeannie said. "We'll leave you boys now, but we will keep you up-to-date on anything we see or hear."

Jeannie grabbed their coats and led Julia to the door.

Once Julia was out of earshot, Lucas said, "Can you believe that woman! She didn't even check for messages or call him before she came running over here. Honestly, sometimes I don't think she could figure her way out of a paper bag."

Joseph stopped him. "Lucas, you made your point very clear when she was here. You know you didn't help matters by insulting her intelligence."

"Intelligence she has," Lucas said. "However, she's a little lacking in common sense."

Seeing Reverend Plain still standing in the group, he said, "Sorry, Reverend."

"I think she's nice," said Angela.

"Me, too," said Joseph's daughter, Emmie.

"Ok, let's get a plan going here just in case she doesn't reach him," the sheriff said. "Dad, could you take the kids back to your place? This could be a long night, and I really want them to get some sleep."

"Sure can," Don said. "Come on kids. Get your coats."

"Aww," Emmie said. "I want to stay here with Daddy."

"Sorry, Kiddo," said Joseph. "Daddy's working now."

"Hey," said Deke. "First one in the car gets ice cream before bed!"

Little brother, Charlie, and big sister, Emmie, both ran for their coats and out the door, as Don and Deke ran after them.

"Is there something you would like for me to do?" asked Reverend Plain.

"Yes," the sheriff said. "I would like you to stay here at the church in case he decides to come here instead of home."

"I will be here until I hear otherwise from you," he said. "I think I will go get a few things from my office before you leave so that I can do some work, but still see him if he comes in the front door."

"Would you also lock the other doors to the building, Reverend?" Joseph asked. "That way, if he does come, he will have no choice but to use the front door where you can see him."

Reverend Plain nodded and left to set up for the evening.

Joseph looked at Lucas. "Well, you've managed to insult two people in the last ten minutes. Perhaps you want to tone down that temper of yours, Lucas."

Lucas ran his hands through his hair. "It's not temper, Joseph. I'm being direct and stating the obvious. She should have called him before she came here all up in arms."

"If it's obvious, you don't need to say it," Joseph said. "As far as being direct, a little of that goes a long way."

Lucas dropped his hands to his side. "Ok, for the moment, let's assume he did take off somewhere. My guess is he wants to get back to Milwaukee. Another option is that he just wants to worry his sister."

"Possibly."

"So, what do we do now?" Lucas asked.

Joseph continued to make notes on his pad. "All right, if we don't hear from Mom in the next five minutes or so, I will put in a call to the station and have El keep a lookout for him when he's on patrol. I would like you to take Angela with you and check the school first and the adjacent grounds. Then, check anywhere either of you may have heard him talk about since he arrived here. I will start looking in places that runaways tend to go."

Joseph looked at his brother and then his sister.

"Angela," he said, "please go in the other room and give Robin a call to see if he either stopped at her house or if she may have heard from him."

"Ok," Angela said, "I can take that in the hallway."

"Lucas," Joseph said, "what's going on with you?"

"Nothing," Lucas said. "Why?"

"You have been rude and insulting tonight. You basically told that woman she wasn't welcome at our table. You tell her she overreacts. You downgraded her in front of her uncle, who is also, by the way, our minister. This doesn't seem like you. So, what gives?"

"She is exasperating, and she doesn't stand up for herself."

"So, your answer is to push her self-confidence down even further?"

"That was not my intention."

"Yet, that's what happened here, Lucas."

Lucas was silent for a moment. "I guess there's a reason why you're a cop, and I'm not."

"Tact?"

"I was going to say patience, Joseph, but your answer works, too."

"Look, I'm going to go check with Angela to see if she has any new information from Robin. I will also tell Reverend Plain we are leaving. Additionally, I will call the sheriff's office to get in touch with El in his car."

"Ok," said Lucas.

"Meanwhile, you go next door and check on Mom and Julia, if you can do so without insulting the woman again."

Lucas thought about an answer; but decided against it.

"I'll get Angela off the phone and be over in a couple of minutes," Joseph said. "Then, we can all hit the road."

On the walk between the church and the parsonage, Lucas's feet felt like lead. He had no desire to walk inside that house and have to find a pleasant way to talk to Julia Garver. Apologies did not come easy to him, and for the second time that evening, he was being told he needed to do so.

He stood on the back porch for a moment before knocking. He didn't know what to say, but knew he had to go inside. Something could be seriously wrong, and he needed to make sure Julia knew that Pineville people, including him, cared.

Julia was sitting at the kitchen table with Jeannie. The knock on the door startled her.

"I'll get it," Jeannie said.

She was not surprised to see her son at the door. She was surprised at which son it was, however. "Lucas," she said. "Come in." She leaned over to whisper in his ear as he passed. "Be nice."

"Have you heard anything?" he asked.

"No," said Julia. "I've sent two texts and two phone calls to his number. So far, no answer." She blew her nose into a tissue.

Her emotions were very close to the surface. Lucas wondered how his brother dealt with people in tense circumstances on a daily basis. He knew it was not his strength. He started cautiously. "Maybe he will call soon, but Joseph is getting everything ready so that we can make a thorough effort to find him."

"Thank you," said Julia.

"Have you called your friend yet?" he asked.

Julia shook her head no.

Lucas struggled to keep his voice level and calm. "Do you think you could do that now?"

"I am afraid to be on the line in case he calls."

"I'll tell you what," Jeannie said. "How about you use my phone to call your friend? I can watch yours to see if anything comes through, and we will certainly hear the house phone if it rings."

Julia nodded and took the phone from Jeannie. "Stephanie, have you heard from Jeremy today?"

Tears bubbled over from her eyes.

Lucas turned away. He couldn't bear to see her hurt. History was what he knew. Emotions he did not. Life had already taught him that he was as awkward with emotions and tears as a fish trying on roller skates. He couldn't mess up again tonight.

"Mom," he said, "I'm going to go outside and wait for Angela and Joseph. If she hears anything, please call Angela's cell. Joseph, El and I will all be driving."

As he walked out the door, he saw his brother and sister coming up the path. "Nothing here," Lucas said.

"Robin hasn't heard from him either," said Angela.

"All right," said Joseph. "Let's go."

Chapter Fourteen

It was only a short distance, but Lucas and Angela took his car to the school for expediency. They slowly drove around the perimeter of the parking lot, looking for any signs of Jeremy. Lucas kept his headlights on their high beams to enhance whatever could be seen.

The school building was silent, with only one car in the lot. Both Lucas and Angela knew that belonged to the evening caretaker. The only lights they saw come from inside the school were from the room in which the custodian was working. Not wanting to startle him by knocking on the window, Lucas typed in the man's cell phone number.

"This is Lucas Anderson. Sorry to bother you, but our new student hasn't been seen for a few hours. Have you seen anyone around the building?" There were a couple moments of silence as Lucas listened to his reply. "Ok, thanks. You can reach me on my cell phone should you happen to see him."

Angela looked at her brother. "I guess he hasn't seen him."

"No, but let's get out of the car and walk around the athletic field and the bleachers. We can't really see into there from the car."

"Should we split up? We can get done faster that way."

"No," Lucas said. "I know Pineville is a pretty safe place, but I don't want you wandering around a dark open stadium without me being with you."

Joseph called the station from his car. "Hi, it's Joseph. Has El reported anything yet?"

"No, sorry," the operator replied.

"Ok," Joseph said. "I'm going to start here at the church grounds. I'll check the church cemetery, the wooded area in back, and the section under the bridge at Main Street. I'll call back after that to see if you've heard anymore. Please relay my location to El."

"Will do."

The Pineville Community Church Cemetery was small, providing resting places for past ministers and a few of the town's founding families. Most former Pineville residents were buried in the bigger cemeteries in one of the larger nearby towns. Stepping amongst the aging headstones, the sheriff shined his flashlight behind and around each of them as he walked. He saw no other footsteps but his own in the mud and melting snow.

Julia was still crying as Jeannie slid a cup of tea in front of her. She was still engaged in her conversation with Stephanie. "How could I be so stupid?!" she said. "I should have known he would try to leave."

"Julia," Stephanie said, "cut yourself a break. First of all, you don't know if he left Pineville or not. He could very well be nearby somewhere. Secondly, if he did leave, that is on him."

"He's sixteen!"

"Yes," Stephanie said, "he's sixteen. He's not twelve. He's not four. He's old enough to take some responsibility for his own choices."

"I'm worried about him, Steph," said Julia, lowering her voice to barely above a whisper.

"Of course, you are! You wouldn't be normal if you weren't. That does not give Jeremy a free pass on this, and that's if he actually left. You need to calm yourself a little bit, at least until you know for sure. Let the sheriff's department do its job. See if Lucas and his sister spot him. Maybe he met a new friend, and they lost track of time. It's not that late yet. There are a lot of possibilities."

"I know, but calm is not what I feel."

"I understand that, Julia, but making yourself physically ill without even having all the facts is not going to help you."

"I don't know what to do, Stephanie," Julia said.

"Do you want me to come out to Pineville? It will take me a few hours to get there, but I can be on my way in less than thirty minutes."

"No," Julia said, "I really appreciate that, but I think I would like you to stay in Milwaukee and see if he shows up at your house."

"I will call my brother and ask him to keep an eye open for him at Margaret's and see if he can take a ride over to a couple of places those friends of Jeremy's go."

Stephanie continued to talk. "Do you know any of those kids' phone numbers? I'll give them a call to see if they've seen him. Don't you worry, Jules. I'll let them know this could be serious, and they are not to lie about it."

Lucas and Angela combed the area around the football field and track. They went up to the announcer's booth first. It was secluded and warmer than being outdoors. Lucas turned on the stadium lights. The sudden glare burst the darkness and stunned their eyes.

They checked under the bleachers, in the bleachers, and every nook and cranny . They found a couple of paper cups, some dried leaves, and a red licorice whip that would be part of the chain link fence until the complete spring thaw. However, there was no sign of Jeremy.

The sheriff saw the bleacher lights and knew that Lucas and Angela were taking care of the school grounds. He headed further back on the church property to the woods that formed a natural barrier between the church parking lot, the playground, the open area, and the river. The wooded area wasn't exceptionally deep. It formed a crescent that kept people a bit safer from the steep drop-off where the land ended, and the river began.

Joseph could hear the rushing of the water. The evening breeze had kicked the churn into a little louder gear. That also meant the water was getting increasingly dangerous to be near. The sheriff knew from sad experience that those who ventured too close to rushing water could easily be swept away in its current. Joseph knew that the waters currently weren't at the danger point, but flowing water always needed to be treated with respect. In addition, someone unfamiliar with the town would be unlikely to know that a steep drop-off existed on the other side of the trees. Falling down a steep embankment could be a hazard on its own, plus add to the water's natural hazards. An unconscious, or even an injured person, would have less ability to help himself. The flashlight crisscrossed the trees, the drop-off, the water's edge, and the water itself. He took his time with the sweep, not wanting to miss even the smallest hint that something was wrong.

Despite his trained eye, Joseph could see nothing from the top of the property. He headed for his car to get closer to a spot where he could more safely get himself right at the river's edge.

Julia and Jeannie sat at the kitchen table in the small kitchen of the homey parsonage. Julia stared at her teacup.

The only sound in the room was the ticking of the kitchen clock.

The sheriff's cell phone rang. "It's Lucas. Nothing at the school. Where do you want us to go next?"

Joseph ran his hand through his hair. "Why don't you and Angela head on back to the parsonage and keep Mom and Julia company? I've finished my search of the river. I'm about a quarter mile downstream. I will walk back, cruise Main Street, and check to see if El has spotted him. If none of those have any results, let's get Reverend Plain back with Julia, and get Mom and Angela home. You and I can take a ride out to a few other places."

"Yeah, that's probably a good plan. Thanks," Lucas said.

"Where are we going now?" asked Angela.

"Back to the parsonage, Kiddo. Nothing yet."

"Oh, man, Julia's going to be so upset."

"She already is, Angela," said Lucas. "Our job is to be as positive as possible."

Chapter Fifteen

Lucas and Angela let themselves in the back door. They had called Jeannie's cell phone to tell her they were on their way back and that there was no information at that time.

Julia looked pale. She was shaking. Lucas crossed the room. He pulled a chair closer to her. He gently placed his arm around her shoulders. "Hey," he softly said. "It's going to be all right. My brother's great at his job."

A short sob escaped Julia's throat. Lucas pulled her in closer to his chest. She allowed herself to stay there for a few moments. The comfort felt reassuring. She sniffed and righted herself. "I'm sorry," she said.

Lucas lowered his arm. "For what?" he asked.

"For not being able to handle my brother, for not making the phone calls before I came running to the church, and for not being in control of my emotions right now." Julia looked into Lucas's eyes. "I'm sorry if I'm not as strong as you think I should be."

Lucas visibly winced. She may as well have sucker-punched him in the stomach. He felt as though the wind had been knocked clear out of his body. He looked to his mother for help. He was so far out of his comfort zone he didn't dare open his mouth.

"None of that matters, Julia," Jeannie said. "We do what we feel needs to be done. You were concerned about Jeremy, and you came looking for help from the few folks you knew in town. There's nothing weak about that."

"Julia?" Angela asked, "I think you're caring and kind, and if Jeremy did run away, it's not your fault."

Joseph had driven to the far end of Main Street. He turned the car around at the laundromat parking lot and was heading back toward the parsonage when he saw a solitary figure with blonde hair and a skater's haircut walking down the sidewalk. Right build, right age. He flashed his brights at the kid and pulled the car to the curb.

Jeremy stopped. He was about to say something when he realized the guy getting out of the car was a sheriff.

Joseph approached him. "Are you Jeremy Garver?" he asked.

"Yes, what's the problem? I'm just walking down the street."

"Your sister is mighty worried about you."

"My sister. She called the police on me?"

"Let's just say I happened to be there when she noticed you were missing."

Jeremy looked toward the sky. He knew Julia worried to excess, but this was ridiculous. "I wasn't 'missing'," he said. He held up a plastic bag. "I was hungry."

"Well, get in the car, and I'll give you a ride home. I'm going that way anyhow."

Everybody reached for his or her own cell phone when a ringing sound penetrated the stillness. The sound was emanating from Lucas's phone, and he saw it was Joseph on the line. He stood up and walked toward the hallway leading to the living room. "Yes?"

Julia, Jeannie, and Angela were all listening to see if they could catch any part of the other end of conversation.

"Yes, I'll call the reverend, and tell the rest. Thanks."

Lucas came back into the kitchen. "Joseph has him," he said.

"Oh, thank you, God," Julia said.

"He never left town, and they are on their way back here."

Relief swept through the room.

Lucas made a quick phone call to the church. "Come on home, Reverend. Joseph and Jeremy are on their way, and everything is fine."

It was only a few minutes before the sheriff and Jeremy arrived back home. When they came back in the door, Jeremy was startled to see so many people in the tiny kitchen.

"What's going on?" he asked. "What's everybody doing here?"

"Looking for you!" Angela said.

"This is unbelievable!" he said. "I just went to get something to eat."

"You what?" Julia asked. "Then why didn't you pick up your phone?"

"Because it ran out of charge."

"Why didn't you leave a note?"

"Because I didn't know it had run out of charge. I didn't see that until Sheriff Anderson picked me up and told me you were worried about me. I told you before, Julia, you worry too much! Now, you call the sheriff on me? Don't you think that's a little overboard?"

Lucas thought the veins in his neck were going to explode. "You had her worried, and now you are blaming her?" Lucas asked. "Why didn't you try to send a text before you left? Maybe then you would have noticed your phone was dead."

Jeremy turned toward the teacher. "I didn't plan on being gone very long. In Milwaukee, stores and restaurants are open past 6:00."

"Well, this is Pineville," Lucas said.

"Yeah, I've noticed. I had to walk almost a mile to find a gas station with some food in it."

"Why didn't you at least write a note, Jeremy?" Julia asked.

"I told you. I didn't expect to be gone long. Plus, I had no idea you would go crazy and call everyone from my teacher to the cops!"

"Well," Joseph said, "now you know that in the future you should either leave a note, text your sister, or better yet, do both. That way, there is no misunderstanding."

Julia looked at Joseph. "Sheriff Anderson, I apologize for rushing over and getting you involved in this."

"You were worried about your brother. I'm glad we found him safe, and rather well-fed, I might add."

"Thank you, Sheriff," said Julia.

"You can call me 'Joseph'. It sounds kind of funny for you to call my mom, 'Jeannie', but still call me, 'Sheriff Anderson'."

Joseph looked at his family. "Well, I guess we can all head home now."

Jeremy made the mistake of saying, "You never needed to be here in the first place. I'm fine."

Lucas was about to say something when Angela yelled, "You know, Jeremy Garver, I told your sister you were smart, but you're not. You're stupid and unkind!"

"Huh?" said Jeremy.

"You have a sister who loves you so much she came to a bunch of people she just met to help her find you. She called her friend in Milwaukee to check with your friends there. Stephanie's brother was checking some of your old favorite places, plus looking around to see if you might have gone back to your grandmother's house. You have an uncle who stayed at the church to be there for you should you go there. So many people were concerned about you and trying to help you. How do you think it's ok to give us all a nasty remark and tell us you didn't need us?" She took a breath.

"Well, maybe you didn't need us to help you find your way back here, but you sure need someone to teach you how to be appreciative!" she yelled. Angela turned and went out the door.

"I'll take her home," Joseph said.

"I can take them," Lucas said.

"No need," said Joseph. "I'm going there anyway. The kids are there. Mom?" Joseph asked. "Are you ready to go?"

Jeannie looked at Julia. "You think you'll be ok now?"

Julia shook her head yes. "Thank you so much for staying with me tonight. I don't know how I would have handled being by myself."

"You would have been scared, of course. However, you would have done what you needed to do, which is precisely what you did. That's all any of us can do."

Julia reached out to give Jeannie a hug. "Please thank Angela for me."

"Of course," said Jeannie.

"Good night," said Joseph.

"Good night," said Julia and the reverend.

Joseph and Jeannie left to join Angela and go home.

"Jeremy, why don't you head upstairs now?" Uncle Wilbur said, "It's getting late. We're all tired. Everyone's glad you're all right, and next time you will make sure you get in touch one way or another with your sister."

"Yeah, ok."

"I think I will head to bed, too," said Uncle Wilbur. "It's been quite a long day for all of us."

On his way into the hall, Jeremy turned to his sister. "I didn't do this on purpose, you know. I never meant to scare you."

"I know," said Julia. "Good night, Jeremy. Good night, Uncle Wilbur."

Once the reverend and Jeremy left the kitchen, Julia and Lucas were alone.

Julia started biting her lip.

"What's wrong?" asked Lucas.

"Other than still trying to settle my nerves from thinking my brother ran away, I am waiting for you to get angry with me and tell me how I overreacted this evening."

"I'm not angry with you," said Lucas. "Why would you think that I would be?"

"Lucas, if the past few days have taught me anything about you, I know you would have handled this whole evening differently than I did."

He dropped his head down and then slowly raised it. "Look, you're right. I would have handled it differently. However, that doesn't make me right and you wrong. We each have our own personality. I would venture to say that my dealing with him would have been a little more patient in waiting to see if he would return on his own, but a whole lot louder when he actually got here."

"Thank you," said Julia. "That was nice."

"It was also true. I admire you, Julia."

"I doubt that," Julia said. "You were pretty straight-forward about your feelings on the matter earlier in the week."

"Yes," said Lucas. "Some people say I'm quite, um, direct."

"So, what makes now different? What in the world would you admire about me, especially after tonight?"

Lucas once again sat down next to her. "It's because of tonight."

Julia gave him a quizzical look.

"Look, yes, I thought you overreacted when you ran over to the church without trying to contact Jeremy first."

"I thought you would," Julia said. "I was scared. I never really thought Jeremy would run away, but I knew how much he did not want to move here. When I didn't see him, I guess I assumed he was taking his rebellion to a new level."

"I understand that – now," said Lucas.

Lucas saw Julia yawn.

"I'm going to head home. Why don't you give Stephanie a fast call to let her know everything's ok before you fall asleep at this table?" said Lucas as he stood to go. "I'll call the custodian to let him know all is well."

Julia stood. They walked to the door together. "Thank you," she said as she reached to give him a hug.

"You're welcome," he said as he held her there.

Chapter Sixteen

Friday morning, Julia awoke to find the following note on the kitchen table, *"Julia, have study group tonight after school. Robin Lee is driving. She's a friend of Angela Anderson's, and another person from the Government in Action study group. We will be at the Pineville Diner. I should be home around 7. (Please don't call the sheriff I'm not back by 7:05.) My cell phone is charged. -Jeremy"*

Julia smiled. "Wow, a note – and some humor. That's been awhile."

Jeremy had avoided Angela, Robin, and Mr. Lucas Anderson as much as possible all day on Thursday. He knew he would eventually have to talk with all of them. Putting it off wasn't making it any easier. He saw Robin at her locker. Of the three of them, he feared Robin the least. "Hey, Robin," he said. "Um, can I talk to you, or are you still mad at me from the other night?"

Robin faced him. "I never was mad at you, Jeremy. Worried about you, yes. Mad at you, no."

"Um, that's good. Angela was."

"She still is."

"Oh, man," said Jeremy, "I really only went to the gas station for some food. I didn't leave town."

"I know," said Robin, "but everyone thought you did, and we were worried sick about you."

"I wasn't looking for people to worry about me. "My sister does enough of that for everybody in Pineville, Milwaukee, and anyone else who might know me." He blew out a deep breath. "I didn't think two apples, a candy bar, and some orange juice would turn into such a big deal."

"I know that," said Robin as she reached inside her locker for her morning textbooks. "I also hear you were pretty nasty when you got home. Nobody needed that, you know. They only wanted to help."

"Yeah, I know." Jeremy ran his hand through his hair and shook his head. "Look, Robin, you know Angela a lot better than I do. What do I say to her to get her to stop being mad?"

"Oh, that's easy," said Robin.

"Yeah?"

"Yeah. Tell her you're sorry, and then stop acting like an unappreciative jerk." Robin smiled, gave him a brief hug, and walked away. "See you at four," she called over her shoulder, "and make sure your phone is fully-charged."

Despite the perky exterior, in her own charming way, Robin Lee turned out to be just as tough as Angela Anderson.

That hug sure felt good to him, though.

Lucas Anderson noticed a distinct change in Jeremy Garver that day. While not raising his hand with answers, he kept his eyes not only open, but focused on the class discussions. He patiently waited for others in front of him to leave the room so he would be the last one left.

Plus, and this one gave the experienced teacher a moment of surprise, he said, "Thank you for being there for my sister the other night," as he walked out of Room 205, and closed the door.

Chapter Seventeen

Julia and Myrtle arrived at the church an hour earlier than usual on Palm Sunday. The palm fronds were being delivered and needed to be set out for the ushers' distribution. "They're almost as beautiful as the lilies we'll have next Sunday," said Myrtle.

"I remember these from when I was a little girl," said Julia. My mom would bring them home and put them in a vase near the front window for that week."

"That's such a lovely memory," said Myrtle. "I lay my palm branch on the dining table. I'll keep it there until I bring my lily plant home next weekend."

"Good morning, ladies," said Don Anderson as he came through the front door with his brother, Deke. "I see the palms arrived."

"As beautiful as ever," said Myrtle.

Next in the door was Reverend Plain, followed by Church Councilperson, Glynnis Oaks, choir members, and the custodian. Julia knew that most people would be gathering on the front sidewalk of the church this morning. This was the one Sunday of the year they met outside, and with their palm fronds in their hands, began to walk as one into the parish to begin their honoring of the Easter week.

Don led the chorus as they came down the stairs from the choir loft in their green robes with gold neck sashes. The coordinated outfits were only worn for Christmas, Easter, and community performances.

Reverend Plain, in his black robe, stiff white collar, and gold cross, joined them in the front vestibule.

Deke, Myrtle, and Julia carried the palms out to the ushers for distribution to all the waiting parishioners.

The procession was about to begin.

After the service, Lucas Anderson caught up with Julia as she was saying goodbye to everyone at the front door. "Hey," he said as he lightly ran his fingers down her arm, "got a minute?"

Little tingles traveled the same path as Lucas's touch. She was surprised at the tender gesture. "Yes, sure," she said.

They walked outside and down the pathway away from the parking lot and those remaining parishioners who were chatting there.

"Is anything wrong?" Julia asked. For the first time since they met, Lucas Anderson seemed more nervous than she did.

"No," Lucas said. "Everything's fine – at least for me," he said. "I wanted to tell you there's been a big improvement in Jeremy at school. He seems to be listening more in class. Angela told me he apologized to her for being 'a jerk' and that they had a really productive study group Friday."

"That's great!" said Julia. "He's been doing better at home, too. He even made a joke the other day. He used to have a really good sense of humor. Hopefully, that's on its way back, too."

They continued to walk along the path, going nowhere in particular, each seemingly content not to rush anyplace.

Lucas stopped. "Hey, do you want to get a cup of coffee or some lunch?"

Julia wasn't quite sure what she was hearing. "When?" she asked.

"How about now."

Chapter Eighteen

There were four restaurants in the Pineville area, with two options for coffee and lunch. The first one was on Main Street, a couple of blocks east of the church at the Main Street Café. The second was the Pineville Diner. Main Street Café, like the Pineville Diner, was friendly and homespun. Unlike the diner, the café was housed in a storefront and decorated in pinks and grays.

The other two restaurants didn't open until evening, Rick's Pizza served the party or sports crowd, while Main at the Bridge served as a more upscale, date, and special occasion place.

After services, churchgoers from Pineville Community Church went to both the Pineville Diner and the Main Street Café. It all depended on where they lived, or where they were going on any particular day. Lucas opted for the Main Street Café figuring that at least they wouldn't run into his family members there.

"Hi, Lucas. What brings you by?" asked the lady at the cash register.

"Just a little lunch with one of our new neighbors. How are you, Vera?"

"Doing fine. Clyde's got the gout again, but he still won't leave those shrimp alone." She grabbed two menus from the stand and escorted them to a booth along the Main Street window side.

"Enjoy," she said as she put the menus on the table.

"What do you usually eat when you come here?" asked Julia.

Lucas shrugged. "I'm not here all that often, but most things are good." He gave a fake conspiratorial whisper. "I'd avoid the shrimp, though."

Julia laughed.

Once they had ordered, Julia brought out her cell phone and sent Jeremy and Uncle Wilbur a quick text. *"At Main Street Café for lunch with Lucas Anderson. Nice to try out another new Pineville location. Will see you soon."* However, before she hit 'send', she amended it. *"At Main Street Café for lunch. Nice to try out another new Pineville location. Will see you soon."*

Their food arrived, and as Lucas had said, it was good. Julia enjoyed her chicken salad, and Lucas seemed to like his Reuben as well.

Julia was unsure if this was a meeting, a regular lunch between friends, or if it was supposed to be a date. Lucas Anderson was full of surprises, and she didn't want to assume anything that wasn't meant to be. "Is there something else you wanted to talk to me about?" she asked.

Lucas put down his sandwich at looked at her. "I want to talk about – to just, talk, I guess. I want to talk about things other than those that make you bite that lower lip of yours, and things that aren't full of runaway teenagers who didn't actually run away."

"Ok," said Julia as she relaxed a little.

"I want to talk about things that make you smile."

They talked for the next hour and a half. There was conversation about Jeremy when he was little, her parents, her Grandma Margaret, her old job at the insurance company, her new job at the church, and there was much conversation about Stephanie.

Two slices of lemon meringue pie appeared at the table along with refills for their coffee cups. "Compliments of the house," Vera said. "Welcome to Pineville, Julia. I do hope you will like it here."

Julia took a bite of the pie. The abundance of soft satiny meringue, the tart, thick lemon filling, and the flaky crust won her over at first bite. "Mmmm," she said. "This is so good!"

"It's the same kind we carry at the diner," Lucas said. "All of us in town get them from the same bakery."

"Where's that?" asked Julia.

"Right on Main Street," said Lucas. "Stop in some time. Maybe you'll meet my aunt."

"Really?" asked Julia. "Another Anderson?"

Lucas laughed a little. "Nope, my mom's sister. She's a Jorgenson."

They walked back toward the church, where Lucas's car was still in the parking lot.

Julia assumed they would be saying goodbye there. She stopped at the driveway. "Thank you for lunch, Lucas."

"Did you need to go back into the church?" Lucas asked.

"No."

"Ok, then I'll walk you home."

"All right," said Julia. When they reached the front of the parsonage, Julia said, "I have a question for you, but it might sound strange."

"Ask," said Lucas.

"This," she said as she pointed back and forth between the two of them, "is a little questioning to me."

"Meaning?"

"Well, I just want to be clear about something."

"Go ahead. Ask me whatever you want."

"Are we friends now?"

"Well, of course we're friends."

Julia shook her head yes and turned to go up the stairs to the door.

"But I'd like to be more than that."

She stopped between the first and second step. She turned back toward him. "Really?" she asked.

Lucas leaned in and gently kissed her. "Really."

Chapter Nineteen

"Did you like the Main Street Café?" Uncle Wilbur asked as she came in the door.

Julia was lost in thought. "Hmm?" she asked.

"I asked if you liked the café."

"Oh, um, yes. It's nice."

"Did you meet Vera and Clyde?"

"Vera was there. Clyde's got gout again."

Uncle Wilbur nodded. "Sorry to hear that. It's quite painful. It's something Clyde has had off and on for years."

He paused a little as he often did between thoughts. "I will have to stop over and say hello. When he gets that, it's hard on the both of them."

Julia still looked lost in thought.

"Is everything ok?" asked Uncle Wilbur.

Julia smiled. "Oh, yes," she said. "Things are very ok."

Uncle Wilbur smiled and nodded, hands folded in his lap. "I see."

Lucas was due at his parents' house for dinner. The Anderson family custom was to have Sunday supper together after the diner closed. This week's would be like most, talking and watching whatever game was on TV. Next week's would be different. Easter, and all other holidays were gathered around a huge dining room table with no television, cell phones, or other distractions. Holidays were for celebrating and family.

The lunch with Julia had been nice. He was happy to see her relax, not constantly waiting for the other shoe to hit the ground. He enjoyed hearing about her past, her family, and how much she liked working at the church. It seemed a perfect fit for Julia, a caring environment where her secretarial skills would blend in beautifully with her compassion for people.

Yet, of all the moments they shared in those few hours, there were two he replayed the most in his mind. The first was the sound of her laughter. It was sweet, like her, not loud or snorty; nor held back in any way. It was refreshing, light and free. He wanted to hear that laugh again and again. He didn't know how one sound so simple could make the world seem all right.

The second was their kiss and the statement right before it. He surprised himself by what he said. He told her, he came right out and told her, he wanted more than friendship. Lucas Anderson didn't do that, at least not in that gentle tone of voice. Lucas usually was a take-things-as-they-come kind of guy. If he pictured himself saying that, it would have been in a pragmatic manner, with no sentiment of any kind attached to it. Yet, there he was, standing in the front of the parsonage telling the new person in town, his student's sister nonetheless, that he wanted to be more than her friend. He groaned. The woman probably thought he was a throwback to the 1940s.

He felt he had no choice but to kiss her after he said something like that, not that he would have chosen differently had he thought more about it. He acted on instinct and his heart. She looked so vulnerable, so sweet, so absolutely... Julia.

Lucas was the last one to arrive at his parents' place, which was a large family home on the opposite end of the property from the campground. Don, Deke, and Joseph were already in the living room searching for what to watch on TV. Emmie and Charlie were running around chasing each other and screaming as kids that age do. Jeannie was in the kitchen putting food into serving bowls for Angela to bring to the dining room table.

"Last bowl!" said Angela as she brought out a dish of hot barbecued beef.

"Well, you got here right on time," Joseph said to Lucas. "You usually get here a good half hour before me."

"Yeah, I, uh, had some papers I wanted to grade," Lucas said as he and Joseph joined the self-serve line at the table.

"Vera said you stopped over at the café for lunch today," said Jeannie.

With the exception of the little ones who were still running around and waiting for their grandma and their daddy to bring them their meals, the rest of the family heard Jeannie clear as day. Each one of them froze in their tracks in the line and looked at Lucas.

"Oh, really," said Joseph. "It's not a school day, and that's usually about the only time you go in there."

"I can't go to the café on Sunday?" asked Lucas. "It's on my way home from church you know."

"Oh, it's not that you *can't*," Joseph said. "It's that you *don't*."

"Let's get our food before it gets cold," said Don.

"Thanks, Dad," said Lucas.

"Absolutely," said Don. "I'm hungry."

"Me, too," said Lucas, grateful for his dad's interjection into the conversation.

"Ok," said Jeannie as she gathered food for little Charlie's plate, "Lucas can tell us during the commercials."

"So much for the reprieve," thought Lucas.

Lucas was hoping the game would prove to be a perfect diversion, and that his lunch would be forgotten. However, for the first time in a long time, none of the Anderson family, including the men, found the game all that interesting.

"Vera said Clyde has the gout again," said Jeannie.

"Yeah," said Deke. "I saw his brother at the hardware store last week. He says this bout has really been a bad one for him."

"So sorry to hear that," said Jeannie. "Deke, you want to drop off some of Don's soup for him tomorrow? You know, they don't make their own soups at the café, and Clyde really likes things he can't get every day."

"Sure," said Deke. "I'll be going that way in the afternoon."

Thankful for any conversation other than his lunch with Julia, Lucas remained silent. He hoped that Clyde's gout was interesting enough to carry them through at least the first set of commercials.

The next set of commercials was spent discussing Angela's school work, and the third set was spent discussing the upcoming Easter dinner. It wasn't until halfway through the game that Lucas's lunch was brought out for family discussion.

"So, Lucas," said Joseph, "tell me about your lunch today."

"The Reuben was good," Lucas said.

"Oh, no, little brother," said Joseph. "You don't get off that easy. There are only a couple of reasons why you would have gone there on a Sunday when you come out here in the evenings for dinner."

"You mean like wanting to get food on my way home from church?" said Lucas.

"Sure, sure," said Joseph. "That's a possibility, but not a very strong one."

"I don't get hungry?" asked Lucas.

"Sure, you do," said Joseph. "However, I think there was a more compelling reason for you to go there."

Lucas ignored the statement. He took another bite of his sandwich and pretended to be deeply engrossed in the truck commercial on the television.

"Did you go alone, Dear?" asked Jeannie.

Lucas knew that since his mom had talked to Vera, she already knew he had been there with Julia. Small town gossip spread faster than butter on hot corn.

He looked at his mom.

"Oh," said Joseph. "You were there with someone."

"That sheriff's job is not lost on you, Joseph," Lucas said. "Can we now change the subject?"

"Oh, no," said Joseph. "I'd say this conversation has just begun."

The game came back on TV. Lucas was thankful but had a strong feeling that the family wasn't going to switch topics after six minutes of game time.

He was right. Five seconds into the tire commercial, the family was right back to talking about his lunch.

"Who was the guest of honor?" asked Joseph.

"Excuse me?" asked Lucas.

"Well," Joseph said, "since you didn't bring whomever it was out here to the diner, I'm going to guess that you didn't want to see any of us at that time."

"I was coming here tonight," said Lucas.

"Yes," said Joseph.

"He already said he had papers to grade," said Don.

"Thanks, Dad," said Lucas.

"Though you could have brought them out here," said Joseph.

"I prefer to grade papers at home," said Lucas. "Less chance of anything getting lost."

"Absolutely," said Joseph, "though there are such things as briefcases and backpacks."

Jeannie said, "Oh, for Pete's sake, Lucas. Just tell us about her!"

"Her?" asked Angela. "Which her?"

"Julia Garver, I would assume," said Joseph, "and I strongly hope you didn't insult the woman again."

Angela let out a huge gasp. "Julia??" she said. "Oh, man, Jeremy's going to pitch a fit."

The good-natured grilling from his family aside, Lucas sincerely hoped that Julia was not dealing with any more temper issues with her brother right now. He needed to call her.

"Got to go," said Lucas.

"Lucas," said Don, "you know nobody's trying to irritate you, right?"

"You've just not had someone in your life for quite a while," said Jeannie. "You can't blame us for being interested."

"Besides, you're picking a good one there," said Deke.

"I pretty much knew this was coming," said Lucas. "The Anderson family is nothing if it's not consistent in its inquiring minds."

"Why the sudden rush then?" asked Joseph.

"It's what Angela said," Lucas replied.

"I'm sorry, Lucas," said Angela. "I didn't mean to hurt your feelings."

"No, that's not it," said Lucas. "I didn't think about her brother at that point. She doesn't need any more stress from him. I think I'll take a ride over there just to be sure she's ok."

"You know the reverend's most likely at home, too," said Joseph. "I seriously doubt he's going to let that boy get too far out of control."

"I know," said Lucas. "However, if I am the one causing her any problems, I will be the one to fix them."

Lucas got up, grabbed his jacket from the back of the chair, and headed out the door.

"Call us when you get home," said Jeannie.

"Yes, Mom," said Lucas. "I'm twenty-nine-years-old, Mom."

"I know that, Lucas. 'Upset' is upset at any age, and once you're a parent, you will know that you never, ever stop worrying about your kids, even if you are pretty doggone sure that they will be fine."

"Ok," said Lucas

After he had left, Joseph said, "Well, we know one thing for sure."

"What's that?" asked Angela.

"She sure has brought out his protective instincts," said Joseph.

"Oh," said Jeannie, "I think you can add a couple things more to that list."

"Such as?" asked Don.

"Vera said he spent a couple of hours with her at the café. It was just the two of them, and according to Vera, Lucas hung on her every word."

"Interesting," said Joseph.

"She also said that every time she laughed, Lucas smiled."

"Smiled?" asked Joseph. "That's been awhile."

"Well, how about that," said Don.

"One other thing," said Jeannie, "while you were out the other night looking for Jeremy, I saw a caring side to Lucas that hasn't been seen before."

"Do you think he loves her?" asked Angela.

"I think that might be a little early to say," said Don.

"I bet he loves her," said Angela.

"Well," said Deke as he got up from the couch to get his dessert, "that's never easy."

Chapter Twenty

Lucas called Julia from his cell phone before he left his parents' driveway.

"Lucas?" she said as she answered the phone. "I thought you were having dinner with your family tonight. Is everything all right?"

"Everything's what passes for normal here. How are you?"

"I'm fine," said Julia. "Uncle Wilbur went over to Clyde and Vera's. Jeremy's in his room playing video games with his friends."

"Are you at home?" asked Lucas.

"Yes, why?"

"I want to stop over if you don't mind."

Julia's heart did a little flutter. "Well, of course, I don't mind."

"I'll be there in fifteen minutes."

At first, Julia felt the joy of her fluttering heart. However, there was something in Lucas's voice that sounded as though he had some concern. She wondered if he was having second thoughts about wanting to go beyond just a friendship with her. Maybe he was concerned about how that would reflect on his job, or maybe he was having second thoughts about her. The fluttering stopped and was replaced by a piece of a headache that would nag at her until he said whatever it was he had to say.

Fifteen minutes seemed like a very long time. Yet, it wasn't much longer when Lucas's car parked in front of the house. Julia had been watching at the living room window since a few minutes after his phone call.

She opened the door even before he was all the way up the steps. "Come in," she said.

Lucas noticed she was biting her lower lip again. "I thought you said everything was fine," he said.

"It is," said Julia.

"Then why are you biting your lip?"

Julia stopped herself. She hadn't noticed she had been doing that. Better to be honest, thought Julia. "I'm concerned about your phone call."

"Why?"

"I was thinking it might be that you were having second thoughts about you and me."

"No," he said with a little more force than was necessary. He couldn't believe she would even consider that, although he knew he had been awkward. "Have you?"

Julia put her arms around his neck. She shocked both Lucas and herself. "Not at all," she said. She dropped her arms back to her side. She wondered if that spontaneous move made her look desperate for a date. "I'm sorry," she said.

"Don't be," said Lucas.

"What is it, then?" she asked. "You sounded a little worried about something on the phone."

"*Worried* is the wrong word," said Lucas.

Julia pointed toward the couch where they both sat. He faced her.

"Look, Julia," Lucas began, "I know you are not used to living in a small town."

"Did I do something wrong?" she asked.

"No, of course not," said Lucas. "However, I should warn you about something."

"What's that?" asked Julia.

"Living in a small town can be a lot like being part of a wonderful, but nosy, family. Trust me, I've lived here all my life, and my family is about as 'nose into your business' as they come."

"Your family is sweet, Lucas. They care."

"Uh, yeah, sometimes too much."

"That sounds like a good problem to have."

"It can be," said Lucas, "but just like a family can be a little too inquisitive at times, and thrive on what's going on in each other's lives, a small town can be like that, too."

"I suppose," Julia said with a shrug.

"Pineville has not escaped that little issue."

"And?"

"And pretty much everybody this side of Wisconsin Dells knows we went to lunch together today."

Julia nodded her head. "Does that upset you?"

"It doesn't upset me at all. I'm happy we went to lunch. I had a good time, and I couldn't care less who knows about it." He stopped for a moment. "At least for the most part."

"Is there an old girlfriend or something?" Julia asked.

"No, well, yes, there are a couple, but they are happily living their own lives. There's zero concern about that."

"So, who is it?" asked Julia.

"Jeremy," he said.

Julia's eyes grew large and round. "He knows? He hasn't said anything to me."

"Well, the thing is, Julia. He may not know right now, but he's going to hear about it. If he hasn't already, he's sure to hear about it at school tomorrow."

Julia shut her eyes for a moment. "I'm not sure how he is going to take this."

"I don't know either," said Lucas, "and, frankly, I would have rather waited awhile before saying anything to him or anyone else. In Pineville, that's not an option."

Julia started to bite her lip again but caught herself. "You know, Milwaukee might have given us more opportunities to go where nobody knew us, but people would find out anyway, I guess."

"Yeah, just maybe not after the first date."

Julia smiled a little. *"It was a date after all,"* she thought.

"So, what do you think we should do?" she asked Lucas.

"Let's talk to him together now," he said. "Explain exactly where we are, and that we had a nice lunch together.

I think it's better that way than if he finds out through the Pineville Pipeline."

"Is that the local newspaper? Why would a newspaper care if we went out for lunch?"

"No," Lucas shook his head, "not a newspaper. It's the local gossip mill."

"Oh," said Julia. She nodded and went upstairs to get her brother.

"Besides, if he does blow up, I would rather be here when it happens," thought Lucas.

Jeremy followed Julia down the stairs to the living room. His sister was nervous. He knew that. He knew her. Yet, why they had to have a discussion in the living room instead of upstairs was still mulling around in his mind. Seeing his history teacher sitting on the couch, perplexed him further. "Now what?" he asked. "Is there something else I'm doing wrong in your class?"

"No, Jeremy," said Lucas. "This has nothing to do with school."

"Ok," he said as he sat in the chair across from the couch. "Then, what is it?"

Lucas took Julia's hand as they sat beside each other on the couch.

Jeremy noticed. "What's up?" he asked with caution.

"You know Pineville is a small town," said Lucas.

"I've noticed," said Jeremy.

"I know that up until very recently you lived in a fairly big city."

"Milwaukee," said Jeremy. "I liked it there."

"I understand that," said Lucas. "The thing is that in a small place like this, everyone knows a whole lot about everyone else."

"Yeah," said Jeremy, "like that you took a walk and your sister called the cops on you."

Lucas ignored the barb. "The other thing is that sometimes people start to embellish things. Not out of spite," Lucas hastened to add, "but because they see or hear certain things and try to put together the rest. Somewhere along the line, that can get added as part of the story."

"Ok, gossip. I've heard of it before," said Jeremy.

"Exactly," said Julia.

Jeremy's posture stiffened. "Have people been saying something else about the other night, because if they are, it's a bald-faced lie!"

"No!" said Julia, "It's nothing like that."

"Anyway," said Lucas, "before you hear any gossip, or stories, or whatever, your sister and I want to tell you what is really happening between us."

Jeremy shot wary glances between his history teacher and his older sister. "Meaning what?" he asked.

"Your sister and I went to lunch at the café together after church today," Lucas said.

"Ok, and now you're holding her hand on the couch," said Jeremy. "So, I take it there's more you want me to know."

"Before I continue," Lucas said, "I want to know if you are willing to stay here until the end of the conversation, and to process it like someone who is not quite, but almost, an adult."

"So, are you saying I'm too young to understand anything other than high school, too stupid to know about life?" Jeremy asked, his eyes narrowing to slits.

"Not at all," said Lucas. "What I am asking you is if you have the adult capability to sit and listen to what we have to say with an open mind and without storming out of the room. I think you have the capability, Jeremy. However, I don't know for sure if you will choose to use it."

Jeremy had a fleeting moment of anger dash through him.

Julia could see it. Experience had taught her what that look meant. "Keep in mind, Jeremy," said his sister, "that he said you have the ability to do this."

"It's up to you if you think you can handle it," said Lucas.

"I can handle almost anything," said Jeremy.

"Good," said Lucas. "Frankly, there's not all that much more to understand for now. Your sister and I have discovered we get along very well. We enjoy spending time together, and we want to see where this will go. While it may not progress to more than a good, solid friendship, right now, we don't know."

"Ok," said Jeremy. "That's the big deal reason for a Sunday night meeting with my teacher?"

"So, here are the parts that I have concern that you will understand," Lucas continued. "While we are not asking for your permission to date, as we are adults, we are asking that you respect our decision to do that."

"Got it, I have nothing to say about it," said Jeremy. "That's much like most of the rest of my life."

"Plus," said Lucas, "I want you to ask us first before you believe any gossip that comes your way. The school can be a real breeding ground for it"

"Oh, great," said Jeremy. "My sister and the teacher. Swell."

"Jeremy," said Lucas, "if anyone gives you a problem about this, or if you hear something that gives you questions, you ask Julia or me. While there may be things we won't say, we will not lie to you."

"Do you have any questions for us now, or anything you want to discuss?" asked Julia.

Jeremy shifted in his chair. "I'm not happy about playing dodge-the-gossip at school."

"I understand that," said Lucas. "Unfortunately, some of that may happen. I can't promise. Hopefully not."

He sat for a full minute, thinking through things in his head. "Yeah, I have a question for you," he said.

"What's that, Jeremy?" asked Julia.

"Can you take her somewhere Saturday night? Robin and I are going to a movie, and I don't want Julia to be home when I come in the door. I think I would like a night without twenty questions when I get home."

Julia's eyes got wide and round again. She was about to say something when Lucas squeezed her hand.

"I think that can be arranged," Lucas said.

Chapter Twenty-one

Because of the many services and church-centered activities toward the end of Easter week, Julia found herself with Monday and Tuesday to call her own.

Although she found herself awake at the regular time Monday morning, she lingered for a while in her bed, thinking about the past weekend. She nestled under the quilt, replaying all the good memories from the past weekend.

A soft buzzing from her cell phone brought her back to the present. She reached over to her little bedside table, and seeing the message was from Lucas, she smiled.

"7:45, kids just starting to filter in the building. Pizza and bowling tonight?"

Julia let out a soft happy scream into her pillow. She made so many typing mistakes in her excitement, she found herself taking five minutes to answer him. *"Sure, what time/where do you want to meet?"* She laughed at herself. She knew a one-sentence text like that should have taken her less than a minute.

Lucas's return message took a regular amount of time. *"5:30? I'll grade papers here and pick you up on the way."*

"Well, at least he's not nervous," Julia said. "Ok," she replied.

She sent a quick message to Jeremy and Uncle Wilbur. "Won't be home tonight. Going out for pizza and bowling with Lucas. Unsure of return time, but don't think it will be too late."

Before getting out of bed, she sent one more message. This one was to Stephanie. *"Wow! Going out with Lucas tonight. Pizza and bowling. Am I supposed to feel like a silly teenager??? – Can't bowl for beans. Why can't a Milwaukee girl bowl?? Isn't that supposed to be in our DNA or something?? Do you think I could learn on the internet??"* She reread her text. "I sound just like Stephanie," she said. She hit 'send' anyway.

Julia spent the morning doing things that normally would not get done on a workday. She cleaned the refrigerator, cleaned the oven, and scrubbed the floors. She soaked for close to an hour in a hot bath, and spent a full half-hour picking out what she would wear that evening. Even so, she found herself with a couple hours to go until Lucas would pick her up.

She tried to read a book, but found her focus wandering far from the plot and the characters. She put on the TV. Yet, even the sights and sounds from the game show's spinning wheel couldn't keep her engaged. She went back into the kitchen. Taking all the cupboards and drawers apart for a reorganization took her until five o'clock. Going back into the living room, she sat on the couch.

Julia awoke with a start when the doorbell rang. "Oh, no," she said. She quickly got off the couch and ran for the door. "Lucas!" she said. "I'm so sorry. I fell asleep."

"I can tell," he said as he pushed the hair out of her eyes.

"Give me just a couple of minutes," she said as she ran up the stairs for the bathroom.

She couldn't believe she had done that. Falling asleep with only thirty minutes until her first date in years was not her best choice.

Julia looked at herself in the mirror. The physical exertion from the day had taken a toll. She looked and felt exhausted. She splashed some cold water on her face. She grabbed her hairbrush and her small make-up bag from the drawer. She did what she could in five minutes. She had already greeted him looking less than ready. She didn't want to keep him waiting any longer. She heaved a sigh. It would have to do.

Lucas stood in the living room, seemingly looking around at the pictures on the walls. Although the pictures were sweet, simple, and typical of an older person's home, Lucas couldn't quite fully appreciate all the pictures of various members of the family during different moments of their lives. He enjoyed seeing them, Wilbur and Margaret at various points in their lives, pictures of what must have been the reverend's parents and grandparents, Julia's parents, plus Julia and Jeremy. However, he wondered if Julia falling asleep meant that she wasn't all that excited about their date that night.

"Sorry for the wait," Julia said as she came down the stairs.

"You sure you want to go out tonight?" he asked. "You look tired."

There was no way Julia was going to tell Lucas how anxious she had been all day, how she wore herself to exhaustion trying to fill the time until he came to get her. She sounded desperate once before. She wasn't about to do that again. "I'm fine," she said.

By the time they reached the pizza parlor, Julia's sleep fog had lifted. She was back to herself. "This place reminds me of a pizza spot near our old house," she said as she took in the red-and-white plastic tablecloths and red vinyl booths.

The thought of the old pizza parlor brought back memories to Julia. The old place had some of the best garlic bread ever. She thought about asking Lucas to order some, but then remembered that they would be in close proximity to each other throughout the evening. Perhaps, anything with too much garlic should be avoided. "What do you recommend?" she asked.

"Well, that depends," he said. "I will eat anything Rick puts together. However, many people aren't too thrilled with that idea as sometimes Rick can put some pretty interesting things on his creations. If that's the case, I'd stick to the basics."

Julia started biting her lip.

"Hey, Rick!" Lucas called.

A man only slightly older than Lucas came to the table. He wasn't what Julia expected. She expected a much older, heavy-set man much like the one who ran her go-to pizza restaurant in Milwaukee. This man was relatively young, muscular and handsome. Julia thought he looked as though he would more likely run a gym than a pizza place.

"Hey, how are you doing, Lucas?" Rick asked.

"I'm good, thanks. This is Julia. She's new in town, and she asked what I would recommend."

"Ah," Rick nodded.

"I think I made her nervous," said Lucas.

Rick turned toward Julia. "You've met my guinea pig. That guy will eat anything I throw on dough."

Rick noticed the lip biting. "Don't worry, I'll spare you the pineapple, cilantro and tomato version."

"Not your best one," said Lucas.

"Tell me about your favorite and least favorite foods," Rick said to Julia.

"I tend to stay with cheese, pepperoni and sausage."

"Is that because that's all you like?" asked Rick.

Julia thought a moment. "Um, no, it's because that tends to make most people happy with the choice."

"Are you allergic to any foods?"

"No."

Rick looked at Lucas. "I'm on it," he said.

Julia and Lucas talked until the pizza arrived. They talked about his day at the high school and her day at home. He left out the parts about how he felt as excited about the end of the school day as the kids did, and she conveniently deleted any references regarding her lack of ability to focus on anything but this date.

While Julia was expecting a regular pizza with sausage, pepperoni and cheese, she was surprised to see a work of art put in front of her. "Wow!" she said as she saw the thick slices of Buffalo mozzarella topping a thin layer of tomato sauce, the fresh basil and oregano, the beautifully-browned sausage, caramelized onions, and pan-roasted fresh garlic. "Rick, this is beautiful!"

"Thank you," he said. He looked to Lucas. "I didn't want to overwhelm her on the first visit."

"You mean there's more?" she asked.

Lucas laughed. "Oh, so much more. This is a modest Rick creation."

After smelling and seeing the garlic on the pizza, Julia flashed back on her favorite Milwaukee pizza stop. "Um, Rick? Do you think we could get some garlic bread, too?"

"You good with three games?" Lucas asked Julia when they arrived at the bowling alley.

"Sure," said Julia. "I need to warn you, though. I'm not that good at it."

"Do you enjoy it?" asked Lucas.

"Yes," said Julia.

"Then we're good." He ordered a lane for them, plus bowling shoes for Julia.

The shoes were as ugly as Julia remembered them. "Here you go," Lucas said, handing them to her.

Julia stared at them. Rented bowling shoes were not her first thought for impressing a new date. "Am I the only one that thinks these resemble clown shoes?" she asked.

Lucas gave her a quick kiss. "Clowns are cute," he said. "We're on Lane 5. I'll be right back."

Julia saw Lucas go into a back room. He came back with a bowling bag containing two balls, a small pouch-type bag to keep his hands dry, a bowling towel festooned with the name of the alley, and his own bowling shoes that were not three colors or ready for the circus.

"Cheater," she said with a smile.

"Why?"

"You look like you bowl on the professional tour."

Lucas laughed. "Hardly. I'm a small-town Wisconsin guy. We all have bowling balls and fishing poles. I believe it's part of the charter for living here."

The first game ended with a score of 189-72. "Are you holding out on me?" Lucas asked.

"No," said Julia. "Are you showing off for me?"

"Not with a 189," Lucas said. "In Pineville, that's about average."

The second game saw Lucas drop to a 171, and Julia rose to a 74. They took a short break before bowling the last game of the series.

Lucas went to the bar to get them some sodas.

"I forgot how much fun I used to have doing this," Julia said.

"I'm glad you like it. Truth is, we will probably be back here Saturday night."

"Ok."

"Jeremy said he wanted you to stay out later than he does. There's not a lot of 'late' options in Pineville. Since he will be at the movies, and most likely not back until ten or eleven, the other option is the bowling alley. We probably should have gone to a film tonight. I didn't think about it until after I asked you."

"That's all right. I'm having fun."

"Good." He gave her another quick kiss.

Julia took a drink of her soda. "I'm not so sure how I feel about Jeremy and Robin going on a date."

"Why is that? She's a great girl."

"I'm just not sure he's ready for the responsibility of a girlfriend. He's just now starting to come back to being himself again. I don't think he can take a girl breaking up with him right now."

"Julia," said Lucas. "You have successfully managed to tell me your brother is not date-ready at almost seventeen, given him a girlfriend, and had her break up with him before he's even gone out with her once. Good grief, give the kid a break."

"I just don't want him jumping into something too fast."

Lucas blew out a deep breath. "Well," he said, "I can help you with that."

"What do you mean?"

Lucas paused before answering. "It's really not a date, Julia."

"Huh?"

"It's really a group thing. There are about a dozen or more kids going. They are not even riding alone. Angela and two other kids will be with them. Plus, Robin's driving. They won't even be in the backseat."

"I don't understand. Why would he lead me to believe it's a date?"

"He said he didn't want you to be there to ask him questions. He's probably got a few of them in his own mind right now."

"Such as?"

"He does like Robin. Angela told me that. Robin likes him, too, I guess, though he does irritate her on occasion. I think they are both kind of working out some of their feelings. Plus, I don't think he wants you to grill him about his new friends, or hear about how they are better, worse, or simply different from the ones in Milwaukee."

"I wish Jeremy would have told me that himself."

"He's a teenager."

Lucas saw some of his students come into the alley. They waved in his direction. He waved back.

"Ready for the final game?" he asked Julia.

"I am," she said. "You'd better look out. I might break 80 this time."

Chapter Twenty-two

The text came through the same time on Tuesday as it had on Monday. However, this time, Julia was still asleep. She didn't see it until nine when she awoke. Her shoulders and back were a little stiff from all the housework and bowling of the previous day.

"I was thinking that tonight might be the last night we can get together until Saturday. I'd suggest the diner, but I know the kids have study group tonight. I doubt they want us to join."

Since she knew she had missed his before-class opportunity to see anything, Julia decided to take a hot shower and put some muscle balm on her shoulders before answering him. She texted Lucas as soon as she was dressed for the day. *"Sorry, slept in today. How about coming over here for dinner? I can make something. Uncle Wilbur has a meeting, and Jeremy will be with the group."*

Julia knew she wouldn't hear from Lucas until his lunch. With Lucas's cell phone rules for his students, he wouldn't take out his own phone either. He might be tough from the kids point-of-view, but he gave himself the same rules.

She ran a few errands to the grocery store, the post office, and the bank. She was back at home with meat browning on the stove when the next text came through for her.

"You don't need to cook. I can bring something."

"Already started making chili. Hope that and cornbread sounds ok to you."

"That sounds great. Hey, how much do you sleep anyway?"

Before she even realized it, she had typed, *"Depends on the dreams,"* and hit 'send'.

"Oh, man," she said looking at the message. She tried to delete it. However, Lucas had already seen it.

His reply was almost instantaneous. *"You can tell me about those later. Also, you have no idea how much I hate to say this right now, but I've got to run. I can't wait for the chili, and the conversation, tonight."*

Lucas couldn't remember the last time he had eaten dinner at someone's house other than his own or his parents. He thought about bringing a bottle of wine but thought that wine might not go too well with chili. He also didn't know if Julia drank. They'd never discussed it. He could probably pick up some sparkling water at the store. However, that didn't seem too festive of a gift to him.

After going through a wide variety of beverages in his head, he switched to thinking about snacks. Potato chips were something for a football party or a picnic. Ditto for pretzels or cheese curls. Those were all solid options when he was hanging out watching a game with his friends but didn't seem appropriate for a dinner date.

Lucas realized that part of his struggle with finding the right match for a homecooked-meal dinner date was that he hadn't been invited to one for a long time.

He went through his mental checklist of previous dating gifts. Flowers were one of his next ideas. Yet, Julia was uncomfortable with so many things regarding relationships. She might think it was too soon for those. Chocolates were always an option. Then again, he wasn't sure if she preferred milk chocolate or dark chocolate. He felt he desperately needed some female advice.

Lucas knew he was not the most romantic man who ever lived. He, like his father and his older brother, were pragmatists by nature. Usually, Lucas was fine with that. Not this time, though, this time he wanted to get it right.

Julia answered the door to see Lucas standing with a box in his hand. He handed it to her as he took off his jacket. The top of the box was stamped, "Pineville Bakery," in gold letters. "Is this from your aunt's?" Julia asked.

"It's one of my favorites. I hope you like it."

Julia took the box into the kitchen and set it on the table. She untied the string and lifted the box lid revealing a beautiful, white coconut frosting. The edges were decorated in a thick white fleur-de-lis pattern. Some delicate lavender flowers were made in ganache and placed on the top creating a spring feel. Julia drew in a deep breath. "Lucas! This is incredible! She turned to him and hugged him. "How did you know lavender is my favorite color?" Julia asked as she stepped back from him.

Lucas looked sheepish. "I would like to take credit for that, but I really had no idea. My aunt recommended it."

"I was never so glad that I didn't make a dessert in my life! This is beyond perfect."

Julia looked through her uncle's upper kitchen cabinets to see if she could find a cake plate. Apparently, her uncle's single life had little need for such fancy serving items. Julia settled for a dinner plate but kept the pretty paper doily on which it sat in the bakery box. She hoped that would pass for a pretty presentation. She placed the cake in the center of the kitchen table.

"We're just about ready to eat," Julia said.

"What can I do to help?" asked Lucas.

Julia did a quick look around the kitchen. "Um, nothing really. Just have a seat and give me a minute to get it all on the table."

When Julia lifted the lid to the pot of chili on the stove, the spicy aroma wafted across the room.

"That smells really good," Lucas said.

"Thank you," said Julia as she presented him with a large, steaming bowl. "Help yourself to whatever you normally put on top." She gestured at the smaller dishes of shredded cheddar cheese, sour cream, oyster crackers, diced onions, and red pepper flakes she had originally placed on the table.

She went back to the stove and brought a pan of cornbread out of the oven. She had already sliced it and had kept it warm waiting for serving time. Quickly transferring it to a serving plate, she added that, and a stick of fresh butter, to the table's dinner offerings.

"You know, if you put much more out here, we're going to have to eat in the living room," said Lucas.

Just before sitting down, Julia hit the start button on the coffee maker. "I hope you don't mind. I usually have coffee after my meal," she said.

"Sounds fine to me," said Lucas.

"I have a question for you," said Julia. "You mentioned in your text this morning that we might not be able to get together until Saturday night. Do you have a lot going this week?"

"It's a holiday week."

"Um, ok. I know the weekend has extra church services, and those will keep me busy. Plus, I know I need to be there late Saturday afternoon and into the early evening when the pancake breakfast people set up the Fellowship Hall, and when the high school kids hide the eggs."

"Who is supervising the egg coloring?"

Julia stopped mid-mouthful. She swallowed. "What do you mean?"

"Julia, this is a holiday week. From Thursday morning until after the last Easter service on Sunday, Pineville is packed full of activities."

"The whole town celebrates?"

"Hmm," said Lucas. "I think I need to educate you on holiday celebrations here in Pineville."

"Please do."

"Can I get another piece of that cornbread? This might take awhile."

Julia handed him the plate.

"Pineville is known as 'the holiday town'. We may have our regular Saturday entertainment in the form of a high school football game or a middle school spelling bee, but come any of the holidays, we are one unified, and you-better-volunteer-for-something, happy place."

"I don't think I've ever heard of that before," said Julia.

"Probably not. We're kind of unique in that way. However, it's special to us. The people who settled Pineville strongly believed that each holiday was given that designation because it was supposed to represent something special, something that sets that time apart and different from everyday life."

"I never thought much about that, but I guess that would be true," said Julia.

"We take those days, and make them as full of meaning, symbolism, and joy as we can. It's a chance to bring people together, bring generations together, bring families together."

"You're such a small town. Don't people have enough togetherness?"

"In some ways, yes. For example, I interact with my family at least once a week. I see many of them at church and at Sunday dinner at my parents' house. I see Angela every day at school. That's great. However, it's our routine. No more and no less."

He got up and poured himself a cup of coffee. "I see my students as my students. I see the mail carrier as the mail carrier."

"What makes the holidays different?" asked Julia. "They're still the same people."

"When we celebrate the holidays, some of those things fade. Each person is a little more dimensional."

"I'm not sure I understand."

"Holidays incorporate so many things. Let's start with the history. At some point in time, that moment, that significance, that event, had profound meaning to someone."

"I suppose."

"So much so, and probably to so many people, that they fought for that moment, that significance, to become something they wished for people to continue to honor."

"That's an incredible way to think about them," Julia said.

"It's the Pineville way, and I happen to think it's a good thing. Maybe it's because I live here, or maybe it's because I teach history and value the good and the lessons of what's come before. Either way, it is how I feel."

"You mentioned how during the holidays you see people in a different way," Julia said. "I'm not sure I understand that part yet."

"Ok," said Lucas, "I'll give you an example you can probably see in your own life, and then I will tell you how it affects even people who don't know one another all that well."

He thought a moment. "What did you normally do to celebrate Christmas?"

"My grandmother would make a beautiful meal for Christmas Eve. We would sit and talk about memories of other Christmases and add in some funny ones about relatives and such. Later that night, my grandmother would fill our stockings, even though we were long-past Santa-age. Christmas morning, we would awake to a wonderful breakfast of ham and eggs. Then, we'd open our presents. Pretty laid back really."

"Same people as usual, right?" he asked.

"Yes, just my grandmother, Jeremy, and I."

"Yet, was it different from other days?"

"Well, sure. It was Christmas."

"So, what you're saying is, even though it was the same people at the same place, it was somehow different."

"Yes."

"Did you do any special things to prepare for the holiday? Did you ever send cards or go out caroling with neighbors?" Lucas asked.

"I'm afraid not on the caroling. In fact, we never once had carolers come to the house that I can remember. We did send cards, though. They went out a few weeks earlier. My grandmother did most of them, but when we were younger, we helped."

"Anything else? Did you ever have any planned get-togethers with other people?"

"My grandmother did a cookie exchange every year with her lady friends in mid-December. Jeremy would get together with his friends one night. Stephanie and I always did something the weekend before the holiday. Plus, the weekend between Christmas and New Year was when Uncle Wilbur could come down. We'd celebrate all over again."

"Ok, so you actually had a lot of traditions that spanned over several days."

"I guess we did."

"Now, let me ask you something about your grandmother's friends."

"Other than one or two people, I don't know much about them, really. I only heard about most of them around cookie time."

"And then?" asked Lucas.

"Oh, brother. Let me tell you, Lucas, this was an 'event'. The cookie baking was only part of the equation. First, there was the organization of who was bringing which type of cookie. They didn't want all six women bringing chocolate chip."

"Why?"

"Because it would get a little boring to eat the same thing. Plus, one of the main purposes of a cookie exchange is to give everybody the opportunity to shine with her favorite recipe, and to let everybody have a nice sampling of different flavors for their families."

"I take it different women liked to make different kinds of cookies."

"Absolutely," said Julia, "having a cookie that people swooned about made them feel so good. All those ladies were retired. They poured their hearts into those cookies."

"Did your grandmother ever share with you any stories about the women?"

"Definitely," said Julia. "That day of the exchange was a big thing for them. They took turns planning it. Some years they met for lunch at a restaurant. Other years were tea and sandwiches at someone's house. No matter where, they sampled the cookies and caught up on one another's lives."

"These women were all close friends?"

"Not necessarily. They all knew at least one other person in the group. Yet, my grandma would come home and talk about each of them like a sister. She'd gush about pictures of someone's new grandchild as if she was going to the Christening." Julia looked into Lucas's eyes. "I remember one year, she came home in tears. I asked her what was wrong, and she told me that one of the women had to move in with her daughter in Florida. She was developing memory problems and couldn't live alone anymore."

"That's hard," Lucas said.

"Yes, but my grandmother didn't really know her all that well. They did the cookie exchanges and saw each other the next year."

"What kind of cookie did she bake?"

Julia looked at Lucas as though he were off in a separate world. "Pecan fingers, but that's not my point."

"I understand that, Julia. However, it is one of mine," said Lucas as he reached across the table to take Julia's hands in his. "For that moment, at that party, she wasn't just the lady who made pecan fingers. She was a friend who was going through a difficult change, and people were able to show her, in person, how much they cared."

Lucas took a breath and continued. "Every day of the week I see the mail carrier as the person who delivers the mail."

"Of course."

"Yet, come this Saturday, he will be the dad of one of the little kids. He will be the guy who will help his son, and his divorced sisters' three kids, find those eggs. He will laugh, and smile, and he will tell no one that he is worried sick about the sister struggling to make ends meet with those little ones. Yet, those of us who know him, can watch him have a good time, and offer him a hand on his shoulder, or some little gifts for the children. No one will care if their package is coming, or their water bill didn't arrive yet. He will be the dad, the brother, the uncle, and a person who tries the best he can to make those kinds of days special for the children in his life. We even convinced him to drive one of the floats in the parade this year."

"Parade?"

"Are you saying you haven't heard about that?"

"I doubt it. What parade?"

"The one that will start near Rick's and make its way all the way across the bridge on Main Street. The one for which the high school kids are building floats and decorating cars as we speak. The one for which the school band will play, the Town Council and the mayor will sit in those decorated cars, the cheerleaders will do their cheers, and the little ones will line up for the bunny and the candy. It's Saturday afternoon, kicking off at one o'clock, before the high schoolers hide the eggs."

"I can add a parade to my list for this weekend."

"Along with the church services on Thursday and Friday, the egg coloring, the egg hiding, and the pancake breakfast set-up."

A look of unease swept Julia's face. "Am I responsible for coloring all the eggs, too? No one mentioned that part either."

Lucas laughed. "No, not the whole thing, but there's a group of high school kids coming Saturday morning around nine to do that. People start dropping off the cooked ones at eight. Someone usually makes sure the doors are open and then chaperones, so the kids don't get too carried away and make a huge pastel mess out of the church kitchen."

Julia let out a small laugh. "I find it hard to picture Myrtle supervising a bunch of high school kids dying Easter eggs."

"I think the kids might have a little more fun with you in charge."

Julia looked wary.

"It really is kind of fun," said Lucas. "However, I would wear old clothes, gloves, and an apron if it were me in that kitchen."

"You could join the fun," said Julia. "I don't mind relinquishing control of the egg coloring."

"Sorry, Julia, my services are needed for the parade. Joseph needs to work. My mom, dad, Uncle Deke, and Angela are all doing something in it. I have uncle duty for Emmie and Charlie."

"Those two are so sweet," said Julia.

"Speaking of sweet, can we cut the cake?" asked Lucas.

Over coffee and the most delicious white cake Julia had ever tasted, Lucas continued to tell her about all of the holiday celebrations in Pineville. His excitement was contagious, and Julia found herself getting immersed in the town's holiday spirit.

Chapter Twenty-three

The middle of the week brought Julia back to work and the church preparations for the holiday weekend. She caught up on the mail, email, and other requests left for her.

Her thoughts turned to Lucas. She didn't want to wait four days to see him. Despite chastising herself over and over through the morning for acting like a school girl, she couldn't lose the feeling.

At lunch, she sent him a text. *"What time are your parent-teacher conferences tonight?"*

During his lunch hour, he responded. *"5:30-8."*

Julia saw the message pop on her phone. *"Do you have dinner plans with anyone?"*

"No."

"Can I stop by with leftovers?"

There were a few minutes before his reply came through. *"I'd like that. 4:30?"*

"See you then."

The afternoon went much better than the morning.

Pineville Area High was in after-school mode. Members of various clubs and teams were either gathered in rooms or wandering the halls. The office staff was wrapping up their workday, while the teachers were trying to catch an hour of personal time before the parents came for the evening's meetings.

Julia went directly to Room 205. She saw Lucas in much the same position as she remembered from her first visit to his classroom, head facing downward, grading papers. "Hey," she said, "ready for some dinner?"

Lucas stood up and took the food carrier from her hands. "Absolutely, the mock chicken legs in the cafeteria this afternoon left something to be desired."

"That was bag lunch day at my high school," Julia said. "They were awful."

"Still are."

Lucas cleared the papers from his desk to set out the food. Containers of hot chili and warm cornbread, followed by oyster crackers, cheese, cans of sparking water, and two thin slices of the coconut cake were set in the center.

"I hope you didn't want too much dessert," Julia said. "Uncle Wilbur and Jeremy liked it, too."

"I'm glad they did. Even I can't eat half of my aunt's coconut white cake."

They talked and laughed as they ate. Every once in awhile, someone would peek into the door, or stop by to ask Lucas a question. Julia was glad to get a glimpse at his world.

The first set of parents arrived ten minutes early for their conference. "Mr. and Mrs. Taylor, thank you for coming. I will be with you in just a minute."

Julia quickly packed up the dishes.

"Thank you," Lucas said to her as she headed toward the door. "I'll text you tomorrow?"

Julia nodded and smiled.

It had been a fast visit, but at least she had a chance to be with him, and that kept her smiling all the way home.

Chapter Twenty-four

Jeremy was putting his morning books back into his locker, when he heard some guy yell his name.

"Hey, Garver!"

Jeremy turned around to see a group of four guys, probably Juniors and Seniors, circling him from behind.

"Yeah," Jeremy said. "What?"

"I heard your sister was here last night," one of them said.

"So?" asked Jeremy.

"Not many people bring a picnic basket to a parent-teacher conference," said another.

Jeremy had never experienced a group intimidation before, and he was quite sure he didn't like it. He also struggled to remember what Mr. Anderson and Julia had told him about local gossip. "And?" he asked with a shrug. "Who cares?"

The group took one step closer in toward him.

"Excuse me," Jeremy said attempting to get past them, "I have lunch."

The boy whom Jeremy brushed against grabbed him by the arm. "Don't push me."

"Move, and I won't push you. I'm leaving," Jeremy said.

Jeremy was about two steps from them when he heard the voice of the one that started the whole thing. "Is that why you moved here, Garver? Your sister got something going with Mr. Anderson?"

Before he realized what he was doing, Jeremy rammed the one with the biggest mouth into the front of a locker. "You watch your mouth about my sister! Got it!"

The other boys from the group grabbed Jeremy. Seeing the commotion, other students heading for lunch quickly gathered.

Robin and Angela saw four of the school idiots gathered around somebody.

"You'll regret this, Garver!" one of them yelled.

Robin ran over toward the fighting group. "Let him go!" she yelled.

Angela ran the other way.

"Robin," one of her classmates said. "Be careful. You could get hurt."

"It ain't your fight," said another.

"I said, let him go!!" she yelled as she jumped on one their backs and hit him with her fists.

"Get off me!" The one she hit was trying to shake her off his back when Angela arrived with Lucas Anderson and two other teachers in tow.

"That's enough!" yelled Lucas.

Teachers quickly separated them and sent the onlookers to the cafeteria.

"What's going on here?" asked Lucas.

"Nothing," one of the boys from the group said. "We're just welcoming Jeremy to our school."

"By shoving him into a locker and giving him a black eye?" asked Robin. "How neighborly of you."

"I'm ok, Robin," Jeremy said.

"Yeah, he's ok," said the loudmouth, putting his beefy arm around Jeremy's neck. "We're buddies, right, Garver?"

"Hands off of him," said Lucas.

"Absolutely," said loudmouth raising his hands in the air.

"What started this?" asked Lucas.

"Nothing started," said one of the guys. "We're just talking to him."

"You four," Lucas said pointing at the boys from the group, "office, now."

The two other teachers escorted the four to the principal.

Angela, Robin, and Jeremy remained in the hall with Lucas.

"Robin, did you see this start?" Lucas asked.

"No, Angela and I were heading for lunch when we saw the Idiot Brigade on someone. I didn't even know it was Jeremy at first."

"So, you don't know what was said, or who threw the first punch?" Lucas asked.

"No, sir. I just know how those guys are. They love to get under people's nerves. They'll do anything for an ego high or a sick laugh."

"You know you could have gotten hurt jumping in there like that, Robin," said the teacher.

"Maybe, but they are not as likely to hit me. They pick on new people most of the time. The people who don't know them and that they're just losers," she said as she glared at Jeremy.

"All right," said Lucas. "Angela, you and Robin head off to what's left of lunch. Jeremy, you're coming with me."

Lucas and Jeremy stopped in the school kitchen to get ice and a towel and then went up to Room 205 and closed the door. "Sit," said Lucas.

Jeremy took a seat in one of the classroom chairs in the front while Lucas sat on the front of his desk. "What happened?"

Jeremy shrugged and repositioned the ice pack on his eye.

Lucas waited for over a full minute before he questioned him again. "I said I want to know what happened."

"Nothing."

"Don't lie to me, Jeremy. I know those kids. Every school seems to have at least one if not many. We have four, each and every one will be lucky if they graduate."

"I tried to walk away, but one of them accused me of pushing him and shoved me toward the locker. That's really all they did, that and get in my face and refuse to let me move."

"How did you get the black eye?"

"When Robin jumped on Chunky's back and started swinging at him, his head lunged forward into my eye."

Lucas knew the situation was serious, but the thought of Jeremy getting a black eye because the girl he liked jumped on some guy's back trying to defend him made him turn around and bite the inside of his mouth for control.

He took a moment to compose himself before he let out a huge breath and looked back toward Jeremy. "So, what did they say?"

Julia's morning had been busy. Between getting ready for evening services, doing prep work for other weekend services and activities, and fielding a large barrage of phone calls asking about all those things, the hours went fast. When the phone rang in the early afternoon, Julia assumed it was another of those types of calls.

"Good afternoon, Pineville Community Church, Julia Garver speaking."

"Miss Garver," said the voice at the other end, "this is the school principal calling. Jeremy is fine, but he has been involved in a student altercation. I need you to come to my office as soon as possible to discuss this incident and how to proceed."

Julia couldn't believe what she was hearing. Things had seemed to be going so well at the new school.

She quickly ran back to her uncle's office to let him know, changed the office voicemail to let people know the office was unattended for the moment, and ran over to the school.

She stopped at the secretary's desk and was shown to the principal's office. "Miss Garver, please come in," he said.

She saw Jeremy's face. "Oh, no! What happened?"

"I'm fine, Julia," said Jeremy.

"I don't think so," said Julia. "Principal Davis, I would like to know what this is all about."

"We all would, Miss Garver. Unfortunately, those four other boys – "

"Four?!"

"Yes, those four boys and your brother were the only ones present when the incident began. The other four are friends, and they present a united story that your brother pushed one of them when they were trying to welcome him to our school."

"And you believe that?" Julia asked. "That one boy would deliberately bump into a group of people to start a fight?"

"Frankly, Miss Garver," the principal said, "no, I don't. However, your brother refuses to provide any other details. So, I have no recourse but to suspend him."

"What?" said Julia. "That's ludicrous! One kid with a black eye, new in your school, against four boys who are known friends? And you are going to suspend my brother?"

"Unfortunately, Jeremy leaves me no choice."

Julia turned to her brother. "Jeremy, you tell Mr. Davis right now everything that happened out there."

Jeremy said, "I can't do that, Julia."

"Yes, you can, and you will!" she shouted.

Jeremy rarely saw his sister angry. "Julia, I'll take the suspension. It's not a big deal."

"Yes, it is, and I am not letting this one slide. You are going to tell him, and me, what happened."

"Look," said Jeremy, "I want to go home, and I don't want to talk about this, ever."

"No," said Julia.

"I told you I don't want to talk about it," Jeremy said a littler firmer than before.

"However, I told you that we will talk about it," said Julia. "I'm tired of the teenage games, Jeremy."

"The *teenage* games??" said Jeremy. "Maybe we should talk about the adult games."

"What exactly is that supposed to mean?" asked Julia.

"Nothing."

"Jeremy," the principal asked, "is there anything else you can, or will, tell us before I make this official? I do want to help you, if you will permit me to do so."

Jeremy was quiet.

"Jeremy, please," said Julia, "say something."

"Ok, here's what I will say. Those four guys are not my friends, were not looking to be my friends, and will never be my friends. They like to goad people into being scared or fighting. I decided not to be scared."

"I do believe that is an honest answer, Jeremy," said Principal Davis. "Can you give me the specifics of what they said?"

"No, that I won't do. I am sorry. I am not trying to be rude. Please don't ask me again."

Jeremy left the office with a half-day suspension, an angry sister, and a principal who understood more than Jeremy knew.

The walk home from the high school was silent. The only words out of Jeremy's mouth were, "I'm sorry."

Julia checked her cell phone when she arrived home. There were three messages.

Message one was from Uncle Wilbur: *"No need to come back this afternoon or this evening. Myrtle is filling in for the rest of the day. Take care of Jeremy, and we'll talk when I get home this evening if you wish."*

Message two was from Myrtle: *"Myrtle Hodges here, Julia. Everything in hand here at the church. Call if you need me for tomorrow."*

Message three was from Lucas: *"I will be over at 4:30. I have to be back here by 5:30 to finish conferences. Need to talk about this."*

Julia was thankful that Uncle Wilbur and Myrtle were taking care of the church office and services today. That was one thing off her mind.

She also knew she really needed to talk to Jeremy. Since Lucas was coming in a couple of hours, that meant now.

She went upstairs and knocked on his bedroom door. She found him lying on his bed playing video games. "Jeremy," she said, "what are you not telling me?"

"I told you I don't want to talk about it. It's over."

"No, I can't let this go without knowing the whole story, and I would like to know before Lucas gets here."

Jeremy shot up in bed. "You mean he's coming here?!"

"Yes, in between school and conferences."

"I don't want him to come over."

Julia looked perplexed. "Why not?"

"Because I don't want him to tell you about today. It was bad enough talking to him. I don't want you to know, too."

"If you won't tell me, maybe I have to hear it from him. I need to know what's going on. I thought you were getting better, but now, a fight?"

Jeremy threw down his video controller on to his bed. "Oh, of course, it's *me*." he said. "It sure couldn't be *you*."

"Jeremy, I don't understand," said Julia. "What are you talking about?"

"Look, despite the fact that I didn't want to move here in the first place, I made a couple of friends. For the most part, I just avoid people. I figure if I get to know them, fine. If not, I honestly don't care."

"I think it's great you have new friends. They seem like nice kids. Over time, you will make even more."

"Whatever. It doesn't matter."

"Of course it matters. Everyone needs to find where they are comfortable."

"You certainly seem to," Jeremy replied.

"Yes, I am happy here," Julia said. "How does that make any difference to this conversation?"

"If it weren't for you dating my teacher, none of this would have happened!"

"What?"

"Yeah, that's right. The 'incident' started because I didn't like what they were saying, or insinuating, about you and him."

"Oh, no." Julia could feel her heart beating in her chest. "Jeremy, I can assure you that Lucas and I have not done anything that would warrant suspicion."

"Maybe not."

"I assure you." Julia thought for a moment. "You remember the other night when Lucas was here, and we talked about gossip?"

"I have a black eye. My memory still works fine. Of course I remember."

"Well, like Lucas said, you have to ignore those kinds of comments."

Jeremy glared at her. "That's easy for you to say. You try listening to people say nasty things about someone you love. See how easy it is for you to just put on the Julia-happy-face and walk away."

"I'm so sorry, Jeremy," Julia said. "I never wanted anything like this to happen to you."

"Well, it did," he said. "Please leave me alone now."

Julia went down to the kitchen, put her head in her hands, and cried.

Lucas arrived a little before 4:30 and ran up the steps to the front door. Julia answered, looking as haggard as she did the night she thought Jeremy was missing. The redness of her eyes told him she had spent a long time crying. He tried to put his arms around her.

She stepped aside. "Come in, please."

"What's going on?" he asked.

"We need to talk. Please sit down," she said.

"Have you talked to Jeremy?" he asked.

"Yes."

"Did he tell you what the fight was about?"

Julia sniffed. "Yes."

"How is he?"

"Mad, I guess."

"About being suspended?"

Julia sighed. "No, he doesn't seem to care much about that."

"Well, it's just a half-day. He probably needed some time to unwind and try to process all of it."

Julia looked at Lucas. "Just a half-day? It's a suspension, Lucas. It's on his record."

"Yes, but anyone who sees a half-day suspension knows there's more to the story. Most suspensions are at least three days."

"Well, I guess I should be grateful for that."

"Is he upset about the black eye?"

"He hasn't said a word about that either."

Lucas chuckled a little. "That doesn't surprise me."

"You find this funny, Lucas? I don't. My brother got into a fight at school because of us, gets suspended, and you think this is funny?"

"No," said Lucas. "Those parts aren't funny at all."

"Then what made you chuckle?"

"I'll let Jeremy tell you that, if and when he wants to tell you. This might be one of those things he doesn't share until he's much older."

"I'm sorry, Lucas. I'm not much in a joking mood."

"Apparently, and I understand why you are upset, but truly, Julia, in the world of school fights, this wasn't that bad. They mainly wanted to irritate him and see if he would cower. According to Jeremy, and I believe him, all they really did is push him into the lockers and keep him there."

"We can't see each other anymore, Lucas," Julia said barely above a whisper.

"What did you just say?"

She repeated it.

"Why?"

"Because it's wrong."

"According to whom?" Lucas asked. "There is nothing illegal or immoral about an adult teacher dating another adult, even if that adult is related to one of his students." He stopped and reached for her hands. "You are not, nor have you even ever been, my student, Julia. We are simply two adults. My job has nothing to do with our relationship any more than your job does."

"I know."

"Then, what's the problem?"

"It's hurting Jeremy."

"Did he say that?" asked Lucas.

"He told me none of this would have happened if not for us."

"I suppose that's partly true, but kids like those four, they find anything just to get to someone."

"It's still our fault."

"Julia, stop it. We tried to warn him about some of this."

"I never thought it would lead to something like this, Lucas. Never." She shook her head.

"Do you want me to talk to him?"

"No, I don't," said Julia.

"Why not?"

"He's my brother."

"Yes. We talked to him together the other night, didn't we?"

"Yes, we did, and I thought that went well. However, look what happened."

"He's a kid. He got into a small fight, which by the way, he showed some guts standing up to those guys."

"So, that makes it all right for you?"

Lucas let out a deep breath. "No, it makes it what it was, a smallish incident, which we all wish never would have happened. However, that altercation also showed him who he is, and what he will do to protect those that matter to him."

Julia stood up and paced the living room floor. After a few walks across the floor, she faced Lucas again. "I can't do this."

Lucas shook his head.

"I am responsible for my brother, Lucas," Julia said. "He has me, only me, and I have to put him first in my life."

"Nothing I say is going to change your mind, is it, Julia?" asked Lucas.

"No. I thought about this all afternoon. Until Jeremy is an adult and ready to stand on his own, I will not get involved with anyone."

"I doubt that's what your grandmother wanted when she named you his guardian. Make sure his needs are met for health, education, and general life? Of course. Look out for him? Yes. Give him guidance? Sure. However, putting your own life on hold until he says it's ok? Come on now, Julia. That's not realistic."

"It's what I feel I need to do."

Lucas stood and held on to both of her arms so that she would stay facing him. "So, you're saying you feel nothing for me?"

"Stop!" she said as tears came flowing to her eyes again.

He let go of her arms and took a step backward.

She stared at him but said nothing.

Lucas started for the door.

"Of course I care about you!" Julia said. "You have to know that! I haven't exactly kept it a secret from you."

"Then please reconsider this decision you are making," Lucas said.

A couple of tears ran down her face. "Lucas, please don't make this harder for me. It's not what I want, but it is what I have to do. Maybe when Jeremy is an adult..."

Lucas held up his hand to stop her from saying anymore. "You need to know I cannot promise you that, Julia. I care about you, and I care about your brother. However, I will not make a promise that I will wait around for years simply hoping that somewhere down the line, everything will align the way you want it."

"That's not what I'm saying."

"Yes, it is."

"I'm sorry if I am hurting you. This isn't about hurting you. It's about helping Jeremy."

"Understand something, Julia. I am not the type of person who walks around with a life on hold. Life is far too short for that, and I am far too pragmatic to play the dreamer who spends years hoping that 'the one that walked away' will come back. I've criticized others for doing so, telling them they were wasting their lives and their time."

"It may not be a waste of time. It could be time is what is needed."

"You have every right to feel that way, Julia. However, I'd hate myself for setting myself up like that. Either I am in your life, or I'm not. You want me to be part of your family, part of your life, I'm here. Right now, I'm here. That's *right* now, not six months, or a year, or ten years from now. I don't play waiting games. If you tell me you're done, then I will respect that, too. I'll leave. I don't, and won't, force myself into someone's life on any level. That's not even respectful. It's certainly not love, and I won't settle for less than that in my life. Nor should you, frankly."

Julia said nothing. She couldn't even look him in the eyes.

Lucas tried one last sentence. "Things rarely are perfect, Julia."

He couldn't stand the pained look on her face, nor could he stay in the strained silence of that room. He left.

Chapter Twenty-five

Good Friday morning brought gray skies and rain. The somber weather fit Julia's mood.

Julia took a long look at herself in the mirror. She saw puffed red eyes, a shiny pink nose, and veins that ran across her face like a highway roadmap. Make-up would definitely be needed for work today. She didn't want people asking her if she was ok or what was wrong, and with what her mirror was showing her, that would be happening a lot if she didn't use every concealer she had.

She hardly slept the night before, constantly waking up with lousy dreams or impatience for even sleep. The tossing and turning, in conjunction with the events of Thursday left her drained instead of refreshed.

She wished she could take the rest of the week off from work and go back to Milwaukee to see Stephanie. She also knew that couldn't happen. It was a holiday weekend, and she had responsibilities to her job, as well as her family.

Drafting a text for Jeremy, she wrote, *"Long day for me at work today. Silent service is from noon-3. Evening service is at 7. I'll be home after that. Call if you need me or want to talk before then. Also, please text me what your plans are for the rest of the weekend as it will be quite busy."*

She sent a second one. *"No need to worry anymore about Lucas and I causing you difficulties at school. There is no longer anything for people to gossip about."*

Julia left for her office before the tears that were stinging the back of her eyes would break free again.

Jeremy saw the texts Julia left for him. "Oh, man, this is crazy."

He answered her first text. *"Day off today from school as you know. Still going with Robin and Angela to diner tonight to study. Tomorrow, I am helping color Easter eggs in the morning and have been drafted into being in the parade and hiding the eggs in the afternoon. At night, is the movie. Sunday, ???"*

He never answered her second text.

Instead, he thought much of the morning about what he could, or should, do. He had a couple of ideas, and he knew his sister would hate them.

Jeremy was in the kitchen when his uncle came in the back door. "Hi, Uncle Wilbur," he said. "I thought you had a noon service today."

"We do, but I want to get some lunch first. By the time I get around to eating supper, it's going to be late."

"Did you want me to make you a sandwich or a can of soup?" asked Jeremy. "I just started making some for myself."

"Well, that sounds quite good."

As he set about making a small lunch for himself and his uncle, Jeremy asked, "Uncle Wilbur, do you think I'm a spoiled brat?"

Wilbur took a seat at the kitchen table. "I wouldn't use those words to describe you, Jeremy," he said.

"How would you describe me?"

"I think you're a young man who's had more than his share of loss for a young age, and who is trying quite hard to adapt to life in a new place."

"And how would you describe me if you weren't a minister?"

The reverend laughed. "I'd say some of the same things, but I'd also say you butt heads with people before you give them a chance. Additionally, I'd say that you are really devoted to your sister, even if you don't want people to know it."

"Do you think Julia is capable of being my guardian?"

"I would say she is honored to be."

"Would you be my guardian, Uncle Wilbur?"

"Jeremy," his uncle said, "why are you asking me this?"

"Julia broke up with Lucas last night because of me. She doesn't think I heard them in the living room, but I did. I was sitting at the top of the steps listening to every word."

"Jeremy, that was a private conversation between the two of them. I doubt they wanted you to hear it."

"Oh, I know they didn't. There wasn't much filter going on."

"You shouldn't have eavesdropped."

“I know, Uncle, but, look, by now, you’ve seen my eye, even though you haven’t said anything about it.”

“Yes, I heard about it, and I definitely can see it.”

“Well, then you know about the thing at school.”

He nodded. “I also know you tried to walk away.”

“Uncle Wilbur, Julia broke up with Lucas Anderson because of me! She told him she wouldn’t see him, or anybody else, until I’m out of here.”

“Did she tell you that, Jeremy?”

“No, she made it seem like they had this great discussion, and they mutually agreed to not date anymore.”

Jeremy brought the lunches to the table. “Uncle Wilbur, I heard them! Julia’s the one that broke it off. Lucas came close to pleading with her to think things through in a different way.”

“I’m sorry to hear that,” Uncle Wilbur said. “I thought those two were tailor-made for each other.”

“I don’t want to be the reason Julia’s heart is broken. I know she cares about him. I’ve never seen her the way she is around him. She’s happy, and she’s usually confident that whatever he says or does, he will make things right in her life.”

“Oh, Jeremy,” said Uncle Wilbur, “Lucas can’t do all that for her. She’s the only one who can make her life work out well. Others may have some good thoughts, but eventually, it’s up to each individual to sort through everything and determine how to make his or her life meaningful and happy.”

“Don’t you think she was happy with Lucas Anderson?”

"Yes, I do. Yet, it's not my decision."

"However, you could decide you would be willing to be my guardian."

"You will be seventeen in July. That gives you a little over a year until you can make whatever decisions you choose without asking anybody for permission to make them. It's also quite likely to hurt Julia's feelings. Are you sure you want to stir all of this up now?"

"I don't want to hurt her! I want her to live a life! All I hear her say is that I am her number one priority. I'm what matters most. That's nice, Uncle Wilbur, to a point, but it's not completely fair to me. I don't want the responsibility for her choosing to live a solitary life or for her happiness."

"So, what are the benefits for you, Jeremy? How do you feel you would benefit from a change in guardianship?"

"For one thing, Julia wouldn't need to constantly breathe down my neck. She's a little smothering. Even Lucas Anderson cuts me more slack than she does, and he's not exactly my vote for 'most laid-back guy'."

Jeremy wiped his mouth with his napkin, took a last sip of milk, and continued. "For another, I won't need to feel like every time she is upset about something that it's my fault."

"Anything else?" asked his uncle.

"Yeah, maybe she won't hate me when she's older and Lucas Anderson never came back into the picture."

The minister closed his eyes for a second before replying, "Julia will never hate you, Jeremy. You need to believe that."

"You asked me a question. I answered you. That is how I feel."

"Ok, Jeremy, I have one or two more questions for you," said Uncle Wilbur.

"Go for it."

"First of all, why did you choose me?"

"Well, I know Julia would never let me go back to Milwaukee to live with my old friends. She would fight that with everything she had. She's convinced they're all hoodlums."

"Not quite that bad, but yes, she would definitely fight that."

"Then, I thought about living alone in our old house. You know, being emancipated?"

"How did you think she would react to that?"

"She would say that we couldn't afford it, and that I am not ready to take care of myself or live on my own."

"What are your thoughts about that?" Uncle Wilbur asked.

Jeremy shrugged. "She's probably right."

"Anything, or anyone, else?"

"Yeah, I thought about asking Stephanie if I could move in with her or her parents. They're really nice, you know."

"But..." his uncle said.

"But her parents probably don't want to raise another kid, and if I were to ask Stephanie, she might start feeling the way Julia does about not wanting to go out with anyone if I am there. I can't take that from two women."

His uncle laughed. "No, I'm pretty sure none of us could."

"So, that leaves you. You're here. I'm already living in your house. I'm getting more comfortable with some people here in Pineville, and Julia won't have to race to a different city to make sure I came home at night."

He looked directly at his uncle. "Plus, Julia trusts you. She would still be able to know exactly where I was, and what I was doing, just as much as she does now. Only, she wouldn't have all the responsibility for me."

"Jeremy, if that is how you truly feel, I think we should talk to Julia. Let her know exactly what you are feeling and why. Sleep on it for tonight. You might change your mind."

"I will sleep on it, Uncle Wilbur, but I can guarantee you I won't change my mind."

Lucas wished school was in session today. Work would give him somewhere productive to put his thoughts. Constantly thinking about Julia would not do him any good. He finished doing the third quarter grades. Plus, he finished his lesson plans through the end of the school year. It had already been a long day, and it was two o'clock.

He made a quick phone call.

"Pineville Diner and Campground, this is Jeannie. How may I help you?"

"Hi, Mom. It's Lucas. You need any help at the diner tonight?"

Angela waved Robin and Jeremy to a booth as soon as she saw them come into the diner. "Heads up," she said. "Lucas is here, Jeremy."

"Oh, great," said Jeremy.

"He's working. So, maybe you won't even see him," Angela said.

"Yeah," Jeremy replied.

Jeannie came to the booth to get their order. "Whoa! That's a beauty!" she said, looking at Jeremy's black eye. "Does it feel any better yet?"

"It looks worse than it is. I'm fine," he said.

"Reminds me of the time Joseph and Lucas were playing softball, and Joseph hit a line drive straight into Lucas's face. That was a pretty one, too."

Jeremy and Robin looked at Angela. She said, "I was little then, I don't remember it much."

"So, what are you eating tonight?" Jeannie asked.

Once Jeannie had left the table, they spread their reference books and notebooks out on the table and picked up where they had ended on Tuesday's session.

They were probably an hour into their study time when Jeremy spotted Lucas behind the counter. "Excuse me," he said to the girls, "I'll be back."

Lucas saw him coming toward him. He wasn't sure in what kind of mood he was going to find him. "Jeremy," Lucas said, "something I can do for you?"

"Can I talk to you?" Jeremy asked.

"Sure, give me a minute. I'll be right out. Why don't you grab that booth in the back over there?" said Lucas as he gestured toward the far corner of the diner. "It will give us some privacy."

Jeremy walked to the booth, and Lucas was about two minutes behind him.

Lucas could see that Jeremy looked nervous. He kept moving his hand positions and stretching his neck. "What did you want to talk to me about, Jeremy?"

"I want to talk to you about yesterday - and about my sister."

Lucas closed his eyes for a moment. He was comfortable talking about the school situation. Lucas was the quintessential teacher, and those subjects, inside or outside the classroom, came easy to him.

The sister topic was a different story. Relationships weren't his forte to start, discussing his with the teenage brother of one of his dates made him extremely uncomfortable.

"Ok," Lucas said. "I'm here. You can say what you want, and it won't leave this table."

"First, thank you for breaking up whatever exactly that was yesterday. I think they would have eventually gotten tired of holding me there, but thanks anyway."

"You're welcome."

"Thanks also for not telling Julia how I got the black eye."

"Did you tell her?" Lucas asked.

"No."

"Does Robin know how it happened?"

"No. She just thinks one of those guys did it."

Lucas nodded. "Understand."

Jeremy lightly rubbed his eye. "Hey. How much did yours hurt?" he asked. "This doesn't feel so great."

"Oh, it hurt quite a bit for a few days," he said. "Wait, how did you -" Lucas sighed. "My mom told you."

"Yeah, at least you didn't get yours because of a girl."

"No, mine is more embarrassing for my brother."

"Lucky."

There was a lull in the conversation as Jeremy stared at the table for a while.

"Is there something else, Jeremy?" Lucas asked.

"Yeah," he said. "I've asked my Uncle Wilbur to become my legal guardian."

"You what?"

"Well, I'm going to go back to Robin and Angela now, but I wanted you to know that."

A stunned Lucas sat in that booth for another ten minutes. "She's going to hate me," he softly said as he stood to go back to help in the kitchen.

Chapter Twenty-six

By Saturday morning, the spring rain had stopped. The sun was peeking through what remained of the clouds, and the skies looked promising for a clear day for the Pineville Easter Parade.

Julia arrived at the church at 7:45 and was surprised to see a couple of cars in the parking lot waiting for her. She was glad to have a fairly steady stream of people coming through delivering eggs, dyes, and other items with which to decorate. It helped to keep her mind off the past couple of days.

Within an hour, teenagers descended on the church kitchen. Angela, Robin, and Jeremy all came in together. "Hi, Julia," Angela said.

"Hi, Angela."

Jeremy took Robin by the hand and brought her forward. "Julia, this is Robin Lee. I don't think you've met her yet."

Robin said, "I'm very glad to meet you, Julia."

Julia smiled. "Robin, it's so nice to meet you. Jeremy has said some wonderful things about you." She extended her hand to shake Robin's.

"Jeremy says nice things about you, too," she said as she smiled back and shook Julia's hand.

Julia surveyed the dozen or so teenagers running around the kitchen or sitting in small groups in the Fellowship Hall chairs. "Oh, my. I'm not sure what to do about this. Groups of teenagers are not my strong suit. As Jeremy will tell you, sometimes I even have trouble keeping track of him."

Angela said, "I've got this. Robin, give them a whistle, please."

Robin let out an ear-piercing one which had Julia covering her ears.

"Impressive," said Jeremy.

Silence descended on the room. Angela said, "Ok, let's get started. We work in teams of two or three per dye set, one decorates with the crayon, one dips. Wipe up spills as soon as they happen."

"Yes, Mrs. Hodges," one of the kids said, which caused the rest of them to laugh.

"Ha-ha," said Angela in a somewhat sarcastic tone. "Anyway, let's go."

Julia took a seat not far outside the kitchen where she could observe without being underfoot. She was happy to see her brother joining in with other kids and to see him smile. She couldn't help but notice his smile was at its broadest when he was looking at Robin Lee.

By the end of the morning, several dozen eggs had been dyed, and many of the teenagers had multi-colored hands. However, the church kitchen was just as clean as when they had arrived. Julia didn't even want to check for fear of how much clean-up she would have to do, but as it turned out, she needed to do nothing except say thank you.

“What time are you planning on coming back this afternoon to hide these?” Julia asked.

“As soon as the parade is over, “ said Angela.

“That would be at about what time?”

“The parade usually takes about a half-hour or so,” one of the kids said.

“Yeah, but then we have to take the stuff back to the school and come back here,” said another.

“We should be back by about two o’clock,” said Angela.

“Ok. I will see you around two then,” said Julia.

Many of the kids headed for the door. However, Jeremy, Angela, and Robin came to talk to her before leaving.

“Aren’t you coming to the parade?” asked Angela.

“Oh, no. I’m going to catch a little rest in between,” said Julia. Truth be told, she didn’t want to see Lucas, and she knew he would be there. Although Julia was well-aware there would be a time soon when she definitely would be face-to-face with him, she didn’t want her emotions getting the best of her in such a public setting.

“Oh, you have to come!” said Robin.

“Well, if she would rather rest-” said Jeremy.

“No!” Robin said. “She will miss you being the Easter bunny! She can’t miss that!”

Jeremy dropped his head so that it was facing the floor, and so that he didn’t have to see his sister’s face just then.

Julia’s eyes opened wide. “The Easter bunny? He’s the highlight of the parade!”

"Yes, he is," said Robin staring over to Jeremy.

"When did you volunteer to do that?" asked Julia.

"Oh, he didn't exactly volunteer," said Angela.

"I told him he couldn't walk in the parade with that ridiculous looking eye of his. I figured if we put him in the bunny suit, he couldn't scare the little kids," said Robin.

"I see," said Julia. "Were you planning on telling me any of this, Jeremy?"

"Nope."

Jeremy's head was still looking toward the floor. Julia took this opportunity to give Angela and Robin a conspiratorial glance. "Well, I wouldn't miss this parade for the world," she said. "I think I will go right now to get a good place to watch."

Jeremy groaned.

Angela, Robin, and Julia smiled.

Julia wanted to stay close to the church to be certain she arrived back there before the kids. She also tried to find a standing spot far enough back so that she wouldn't be completely visible to the crowd, but still close enough that she could see the parade itself. She stood behind some grandparents and partially behind a large elm tree.

She spotted Lucas about a half-block down on the other side of the street. A lump formed in her throat as she watched him settle Emmie and Charlie on a blanket on the curb. He was so caring, so kind.

She forced herself to look in a different direction. She had made her decision, and she believed it was the right one.

Thankfully, the parade began, and Julia was caught up in the sweetness of it. Hand-decorated floats and cars were all decked out in spring colors. Julia wondered if there was any crepe paper left on store shelves within thirty miles.

The first person she saw that she knew was Glynnis Oaks, riding in the Town Council car. Glynnis spotted her in the crowd and waved. "Hi, Julia!" she said.

Julia waved back and positioned herself still a little further behind the tree.

One of the cars was from the Pineville Diner and Campground. The decorations included very miniature pine trees in the flatbed of the old truck. Deke was driving, while Jeannie and Don waved to the crowd and handed out diner coupons.

There were floats from each one of the high school classes, cars from many of the local businesses and government offices, and the mayor's car was driven by a beaming man who clearly was enjoying his part in the celebration. Julia wondered if that was the mail carrier Lucas had mentioned.

Julia saw the cheerleaders coming down Main Street waving their pom pons in unison. "Gooooo, 'Jacks'!" they yelled, referencing the Pineville Area High School team name, the Lumberjacks. One of the loudest and perkiest of the cheerleaders was none other than Robin. Julia smiled again. When her brother was at his surliest, he would never have dated a cheerleader, much less let himself be talked into dying eggs or being dressed up in a bunny suit.

Shortly after the cheerleaders came the school band, and Julia spotted a familiar-looking clarinet player in Angela Anderson.

A few more cars and floats later came the grand finale of the parade. The Senior-class float held the star of the parade, the Easter bunny. Julia whooped and cheered in a way that would make Stephanie proud. She regained a bit of her composure. "I love you, Easter Bunny," she said in a quiet voice.

The afternoon went well for Julia as she took her same chair while the high school group hid Easter eggs inside and outside the church.

"Don't hide them too well, especially inside," Angela said. "We want the littlest kids to be able to find some. Plus, we don't want to find them when they start to go bad. A church that smells like rotten eggs would not be a good thing."

Myrtle Hodges had the timing down to a science. About the time the high schoolers were leaving, the Pancake Breakfast set-up people appeared. Roughly an hour after the breakfast crew arrived, everything was ready for the next day, and Julia could go home.

She was hoping to relax.

Chapter Twenty-seven

Julia came in to the kitchen to see Jeremy in what appeared to be deep thought. "Everything all right?" she asked.

"I'll wait for Uncle Wilbur to come home," he said.

"Is it something important?" Julia asked.

"Yeah, but I don't want you to overreact."

"What is it?" she asked. "Is your eye hurting you?"

"My eye will be fine," Jeremy said. "Can't you let it go?"

"I don't understand," Julia said. "You used to be able to talk to me. Why can't you now?"

"Because I've never had to tell you anything like this before. I've never had to tell anybody anything even close."

Julia sat on the chair next to him. "Now you're starting to worry me. I think we'd better talk. Whatever it is, anytime in your life, I want you to feel you can tell me."

"I don't know how."

"Please don't shut me out, Jeremy. I only want to help you."

The pleading look in his sister's eyes was more than Jeremy could handle. "I have asked Uncle Wilbur if he will be my guardian."

Julia gasped. "Jeremy, no! If this is about the fight the other day-"

"It's about everything. You worry about me too much, and I know I don't always make it easy on you."

"You're a kid. It's not your job to make my life easier. I'm the adult. That's my job."

"Not anymore. Uncle Wilbur will take over that part. You don't have to worry about me."

"Look, I know I don't always do everything right, but I try. Ok? I really do try."

"I know that, Julia."

"You've already talked to Uncle Wilbur?"

"Yes, and he will do it if you will agree."

"This is what you really want?"

"Yes."

"So, you want me out of your life? You and he want me to move out?"

"No," Jeremy said. "I don't want you out of my life. Nobody wants you to move. I just think Uncle Wilbur is better suited for some of it. He's older. He's dealt with teenagers in all sorts of ways, and he doesn't get worked up like you do."

"Well, I'm sorry about that. I am who I am, Jeremy. I cannot promise you that I will look the other way every time you don't want to talk to me, or something important happens. That's one thing I cannot do, not even, no, especially, for you."

"I want you to be my sister again, Julia, not my guardian, or my substitute mom or grandma, just my sister."

"You've dropped quite a bombshell here. I'm going to need some time to think it through."

"Please think about it, Julia. It means a lot to me."

Julia nodded and went upstairs to her room. She didn't think today could be any worse than yesterday, but somehow, it just got there.

Shortly after she heard her brother leave the house, Julia dialed Stephanie's number.

"Hey, Jules, how are things?" Stephanie asked. "How's Bro-Bro? How's small-town living? How's the handsome new love?"

"Not great," Julia answered.

"To which question?"

"All of them."

"Uh-oh," Stephanie said. "What's happening out there? The last time I heard from you, things were going so much better. Can I help?"

After about a half-hour of Stephanie listening to Julia talk about everything that had transpired in the last couple of days, Julia took a breath and asked her best friend what she thought about all of it.

"Wow, Jules," she said. "I'm not sure what to think. If Jeremy's improving overall, maybe you want to ride with that. That was one of your main concerns when you left here, right?"

"This hurts, Stephanie."

"I'm sure it does, in more ways than one."

"Yes, I admit that, but only to you, Steph. I cannot let anyone else know how I feel."

"Why? Why not tell them all? Jeremy, your uncle, Lucas? They all deserve to know how you feel, and you deserve to get it off your chest."

"I'm doing that right now, Stephanie."

"Yeah, to me you are. I'm your friend, but I am not one of the people who will be directly impacted by whatever decisions you either recently made or are about to make."

"My head is spinning with all of this."

"Listen, Julia, search your heart, really, really deep. Look at all of the stuff that's in there, whether you want to do so or not. Then, make your decisions."

"Maybe later. I've got a splitting headache."

"Ok," Stephanie said. "I'm going to let you go and get some rest. However, please don't make a final decision at least until you talk to your uncle. I know how fond he is of you, and how proud he is of all you've undertaken. Please see if there is something else going on here."

"We'll see," said Julia. "I've talked so much the last few days. All I want to do now is sleep and hope this all goes away."

"That's unlikely to happen."

"I know."

"So, promise me you will talk to your uncle, or I am getting in my car right now."

"Don't do that. I'm twenty-five. I need to learn to make decisions without relying on someone to prop me up so I don't keel over from fear."

"Would you rather start by talking to Lucas?" Stephanie asked.

"No!"

"Then talk to Wilbur."

"Fine, if and when the subject comes up. Maybe Jeremy will change his mind."

"And maybe he won't. Find out why."

Julia did not need to make any decisions that evening as to which conversation to have first. Exhaustion caught up with her. She fell asleep, in her clothes, before six in the evening. She never heard her uncle come home. She never heard Jeremy come home. The last thing she did was to lie down for what she thought would be a few minutes when she hung up from talking with Stephanie.

Her alarm went off at five a.m. on Easter Sunday morning. Sunrise Service began in one hour.

Chapter Twenty-eight

The sanctuary of the church was a sea of white. Lilies, bought and donated by the parishioners for this special day, ringed the front. The soft floral scent wafted back a few rows. The white Easter cloth on the pulpit, that crisp clean color that signifies purity and beginning, was yet another sign of the change in the church year.

Those in attendance were dressed in full holiday clothes. More women than usual wore dresses. More men than usual dressed in suits. Young boys looked like uncomfortable miniature versions of their fathers, pulling at the neck bands of their kid-sized ties. Many of the little girls had frilly dresses, patent leather shoes, and lacy little socks or gloves. It took Julia back in time to her church as a young girl. Even with as sad as she was, she appreciated the beauty and sweetness of it all.

The choir's opening anthem was full of alleluias and majesty. One of the high school boys played his trumpet on another song, and by the end of the service, people departed the sanctuary for the Fellowship Hall breakfast, many with happy faces and uplifted spirits.

Julia planned on walking straight into the church kitchen to busy herself in the back and away from everyone, but particularly the Anderson family. She truly cared for all of them but could not bring herself to sit at the same table right now.

She felt a stabbing, permeating sadness. It wasn't going to improve if she sat next to the man she already knew she loved but probably would never have. She couldn't do it. She was thankful to see out of the corner of her eye that the entire family was engrossed in conversation and didn't notice her.

Her one fear in getting to the kitchen unnoticed was if one of them started a conversation with her. Julia also knew she didn't have it in her to be rude or abrupt with any of them. From the oldest Anderson, Deke, to the youngest, Charlie, every single one of them had been kind to her.

Thankfully, she was able to avoid eye contact. Julia slipped into the kitchen and put on an apron. She set herself up at the kitchen sink and started washing the many used dishes that seemed to magnify throughout the next hour.

She finished up as the youngsters were involved in the egg hunt, which was what she had hoped would happen.

Julia made her way to the back-left corner of the church for the final service of the day. She knew the Anderson family always sat on the right half, near the front. It was too early for anyone else to have come into the sanctuary for the service. Julia bowed her head, prayed, and read the church bulletin over-and-over again.

Lucas knew Julia had to be there. He had looked around as much as he could at the breakfast but didn't see her. He checked her office but found no one in there other than an usher dropping off a note. He checked the choir loft, nobody. He checked the parking lot as the little ones were off gathering eggs. She wasn't there either. He would have checked the kitchen, but it was packed full of Easter breakfast volunteers.

He went back to the egg hunt area. Charlie and Emmie were returning with little baskets full of colorful eggs.

"Look, Uncle Lucas," Emmie said. "Charlie found the glitter one with all the gold and silver sparkles on it!"

"Wow," said Lucas. "That's really special, Charlie. The bunny only brings one of those each year."

"I show it to Ju-wee-uh," the little boy said.

Lucas looked as though the little guy had punched him square in the stomach.

"Maybe we can do that later, Charlie," Jeannie said.

At the end of the egg hunt, it was announced that the most eggs were found by eight-year-old Lindsay Luggins, and that Charlie Anderson found this year's Glitter Egg. People cheered, and nobody mentioned that Lindsay had actually taken half of her kid brother's eggs and mixed them in with hers to win the three-inch plastic statue.

The final service of the Easter church celebration was about to begin. All of the egg-hunters and their families joined the rest of the people who were making their way back inside the church building.

Lucas did a quick scan of the crowd as he walked toward the front. He still did not see Julia.

Reverend Plain delivered a beautiful sermon on the significance of Easter in the church and the beauty of this season. He spoke of God's forgiveness and love for each person. He spoke of the newness Easter brought to the church. He then brought the message to the congregants that, even in their imperfect humanity, they should act as God-like as possible, showing forgiveness and love to each other. He spoke of each and every day allowing for new beginnings in all lives.

The service ended with another beautiful song from the choir.

As he was leaving the sanctuary, Lucas spotted Julia in the back corner. "I'll meet you at the house in a little bit," he said to his family as he tried to get as quickly as possible to the other section.

He waited until the very end of the crowd.

She spotted him waiting for her. She shook her head no, and turned back around to go back to her uncle's office.

That was all Lucas needed to see. From the look on her face he could tell that Jeremy had made his wishes known, and Lucas believed as he did the day before, that she hated him for it.

Julia sat in her uncle's office until he came back from wishing his congregants a Happy Easter.

"Julia," he said as he opened the office door, "What brings you in here?"

"I talked to Jeremy yesterday," she said. "He told me he wants you to take over as guardian."

"Oh," said her uncle. "I thought we agreed we would do that when we were all home together."

"Well, don't blame him for that. I pretty much forced it out of him. I was worried about what was going on in his mind." She stood up and faced the wall toward the pictures. "I guess now I know."

"How are you holding up? You've had quite a rough few days."

"That's certainly true," she said as she turned back to face him. "I knew I wasn't doing the best job with him, and that I needed some help. I didn't think I was so bad at it that he would want someone else."

"Uh-huh," said the reverend. "Julia, what exactly did Jeremy tell you?"

"He said that you agreed to do this if I said I was ok with it, and that I don't let go of things with him."

"Dear child," he said. "You are missing an important section of this, and it's one you need to know."

"I don't know how much more I can take this week, but if you think I should hear it, tell me."

"Julia, Jeremy is concerned about you."

"What?" she stopped. "Why?"

"He thinks you are living your life only based on him."

"Well, I guess I can see that, but even if I wasn't legally responsible for him, I would still worry. He's my brother."

"True, but would you worry as much?"

Julia bit her lower lip. "I don't know."

"Would you have moved out here to Pineville?"

"I don't know that either, but I'm glad I did. I like it here."

"That's good," Uncle Wilbur said. "Tell me, would you have ended your relationship with Lucas Anderson?"

Julia sat up ramrod straight in the chair. "I did what I thought was best for Jeremy."

"And he is doing what he thinks is best for you. Jeremy feels as responsible for your happiness as you do for his."

"That's not his job to do that! He's still a teenager!" Julia said.

"Nevertheless, he does, and you refusing to live your life the way you otherwise would bothers him."

"What do I do, Uncle Wilbur?"

"Julia, this is a decision I cannot make for you. It's only you that knows what you feel inside. While all the rest of us have a part in your life, it is indeed your life. If you want to end the legal responsibilities with Jeremy, both he and I will understand that. Very few women of your age must handle parenting a teenager. I will step in if that is both yours and Jeremy's requests."

"No, I don't want to do that, and it's not a matter of pride. It's a matter of commitment and of love. I couldn't bear to take myself out of that."

"If you need help, it is not a sign of failure to ask for it. Wise people know when to ask for reinforcement."

"I came here so I could have some help."

"You must ask yourself, Julia, if what I have given you up until now is enough assistance for you. Is it the right kind of assistance for you? You must also ask yourself if it's enough for Jeremy. Those are hard questions to ask head-on."

"Oh, I just don't know!"

"Besides which, you better ask yourself one more thing," her uncle said.

"What's that?"

"I saw a very dejected man walking out of this church this morning. He wanted to talk to you."

"I can't talk to Lucas right now," said Julia.

"Why not?"

"It's hard, Uncle Wilbur."

"Anything of value is."

"It's complicated."

"I don't know of one thing in life that isn't. Yet, here's the thing about all this. Refusing to look deep inside, and not wanting to face the tough things make them even tougher. Tough questions don't answer themselves."

Chapter Twenty-nine

There was a knock at Julia's bedroom door. "Julia?" Jeremy asked.

"Yes, come on in," she said.

"Can you give me a ride out to the Andersons?"

"You're kidding me, right?"

"No, I need a ride."

"On Easter Sunday? I thought the diner was closed on Sunday nights."

"It is, but I am going to the house. Robin is over there for dinner, and they invited me, too."

"I was just about to put a ham in the oven."

"Well, make it for yourself when you get back."

"It will be for myself. Uncle Wilbur went to visit some of the house-bound parishioners. He says the holidays can be exceptionally lonely for them."

"You ok with being here alone on Easter?"

"I suppose so," said Julia. "Why didn't Robin give you a ride over there?"

"She only planned on being there for an hour or so, but they invited her to stay, and now they invited me."

Julia massaged her forehead. "I don't know, Jeremy. I'm not sure I'm up to seeing them right now."

"Then drop me off in the diner parking lot, and I'll walk from there. Robin will give me a ride home."

Julia heaved a huge sigh. "All right," she said.

She pulled into the empty, diner parking lot. "I don't feel comfortable letting you out here," Julia said.

"Why not?" asked Jeremy.

"It's deserted with the diner being closed."

"Oh, for Pete's sake, Julia," he said. "I'm almost seventeen. However, if you feel like I might get accosted by that phantom pine tree over there, you can drive over to the house. It's off to the left on that dirt road over there."

Julia started down the single-lane, dirt road. About a block or so into the path, another car was coming the opposite way. "Great," she said. "Now what do I do?"

"Pull off by that gap there and let him pass," said Jeremy.

Julia maneuvered her car onto the little patch of grass between some pine trees. As the oncoming car came closer, she recognized it as Lucas's. "Not who I wanted to see," she said.

As Lucas slowed his car to see who else was on the private road, he saw it was Julia's car. He stopped as he approached and got out to talk to her.

Jeremy jumped out of the car. "I'll take it from here. The house is right past that next incline." He waved to Lucas as he ran past him.

Lucas came to Julia's driver-side window and motioned for her to roll it down.

She hesitated, but she did. "Hi," she said.

"Happy Easter," said Lucas.

"Thanks, to you and your family, too."

"Why wouldn't you talk to me at the church this morning? I felt like an idiot standing there and you walking the other way."

"I had a lot on my mind."

"We all do," he said. "Look, I've got to run to the diner and bring back some ice to the house. Will you go with me and let me know what's been going on the last couple of days? I was worried about you after Jeremy told me he asked you to give the guardianship to your uncle."

Julia turned off her ignition, got out of her car, and got into Lucas's.

"When did he tell you that?"

"Friday night at the diner."

"Some guardian and big sister I am. I have a brother who is surer of himself than I am."

"I'm sorry if him doing that has anything to do with me," Lucas said. "I would never ask you to make any kind of a decision that would pull you out of your brother's life."

"I'm not leaving his life, and I'm not turning over guardianship to my uncle."

Lucas shook his head. "Understood. You were quite clear where your priorities were."

They pulled directly to the back door of the diner. Lucas jumped out. "I'll be back in a minute."

He returned with a very large bag of ice thrown over his shoulder.

"How many people are at your parents' house?" Julia asked.

"Probably a couple of dozen. I stopped counting at eighteen."

"That's quite a group," Julia said.

"It's a holiday. It's Pineville. Put them together, lots of people."

They were back at her car. "Look, there's a whole group of people in that house. Why don't you stay for dinner, too?"

"I'm not sure that's a good idea," said Julia.

"You wouldn't even have to talk to me if you don't want," Lucas said. "The family misses you. The little ones wanted to show you their eggs at church after the hunt, but you were nowhere to be seen."

"I'm sorry about that."

"Do you dislike my family now as well? Is that going to be part of the silent treatment?"

Julia face became quite flushed. "Lucas Anderson, are you out of your mind?" she asked. "I love those people! They are some of the nicest people I've ever met. It's breaking my heart not to talk to them."

"Then why didn't you?"

"Because you were there."

"Wow, when you hate someone, you really pour your all into it. Don't you?"

"I don't hate you!"

"There's just no room in your life for me. Is that it?"

"I want you in my life."

"How? You told me the other night we couldn't continue to see each other. I thought at least we could maintain civility with one another or be some sort of friends."

Julia was quiet for a moment. "Lucas, I want to tell you a few decisions I've made in the last couple of days that have nothing to do with our relationship. Will you listen?"

"Sure."

"First, I've already told you that I am not giving up my guardianship."

"You said that."

"However, I am going to be sharing more of the responsibilities with my uncle. Jeremy can decide which one of us he may feel most comfortable approaching in any given circumstance. If Uncle Wilbur or I feel the other person needs to know, we will share that. I've gotten the impression in the last few days that Jeremy is sometimes more comfortable talking to a man about certain things rather than his sister."

"That would be normal," Lucas said.

"So, it took me awhile to figure that out. I sometimes still see him as a little boy."

"I've noticed."

"The second thing concerns you and him, and I told Jeremy that I would talk to you when we next spoke." Julia looked at Lucas. "I guess that's today."

"Go ahead. What is it?"

"Well, he asked if he needed a man's advice who was not his older great-uncle, the minister, if he could come to you. Would you be ok with that?"

"Of course, but Julia, you and I don't always see things the same way. Will you be ok with that? If you want me to do that, I will say what I feel, not necessarily what you think I should say."

"It took some thinking, but yes. I am."

"Anything else?" asked Lucas as she started to get out of his car for hers.

"Yes, I decided to go back to an old boyfriend-"

"Hold it," said Lucas. "You told me we couldn't date because you had all of these responsibilities. Was that a convenient excuse?"

"You know me better than that."

"I thought I did," said Lucas. "Then who is this guy, and how strong of a relationship was it that it's pulling you back?"

"He's a guy who says what I need to hear, even when I don't want to hear it."

"Common sense guy or an arrogant one?"

"He can be both. Sometimes he thinks he has all the answers, not only some of them."

"Hm."

"He's very good looking."

"Like I would care about that. He's probably got an ego to match."

"Sometimes, but he's usually pretty sweet."

"How does he treat you?"

"Quite well, but I know I frustrate him."

"How is he with Jeremy?"

"Oh, Jeremy hated him when we first got together."

"Not sure I like him or that he's right for you."

"Really?" asked Julia. "I was hoping you would give us your blessing to continue."

Lucas looked at her as though she told him her space ship just landed. "You want me to what? Julia, you don't ask much, do you?" He stared at her. "Date who you want," he said with more than a little tone.

Julia sat back down and closed the car door. "Lucas," she said, "has anyone told you that you are a little slow to figure things out?"

She leaned over to his side of the car and kissed him.

Chapter Thirty

A few minutes later, Lucas said, "I think I had better get back with that ice now."

Julia started to get out of his car.

"You're coming to dinner, too."

"Are you sure that your family will want me there?"

Lucas shook his head. "You know, Julia, you're pretty slow at figuring things out, too."

The party was in full swing when Lucas and Julia arrived back at the house. Julia knew many, but not all, of them. She saw Jeremy sitting with his arm around Robin's shoulders, and Julia quickly looked the other way to avoid embarrassing him. Deke raised his glass to her as if offering a toast. Hellos came wherever she looked.

A little bundle of toddler-energy came running to her. "Ju-wee-uh!" he said as he threw his arms around her knees.

"Hey, Charlie, I heard you found the most special egg today," she said. "That's great, Kiddo!"

Charlie took her hand and started pulling her. "You come see. You come see!"

The rest of the night past in a pleasant blur of good food and even better conversation. Julia couldn't remember a more eventful, and pleasant, holiday.

Later that night, as she lay in bed still smiling at all that had happened, Julia called Stephanie. "Happy Easter, Steph!" she said. "How did your day go with your family?"

"It was good, Jules. Mom made leg of lamb. Dad spilled half the gravy boat on his tie. My brother managed to get the day off from work, so he was there. You know. It was nice. How was yours?"

"Oh, Stephanie," Julia said. "I don't know where to start. It's been a busy, crazy, heartbreaking, heartwarming, overwhelming, so-glad-I-was-here, holiday."

"What's that supposed to mean?"

Julia laughed. "You'll have to come out here to truly know, but for now let's just say it was 'A Pineville Easter'."

About the Author

I am a wife, mother, grandmother, daughter, sister, aunt, niece, friend, - and writer. I am grateful for my faith, my family, and my friends, plus all other people, places, moments, and things that have brought joy into my life.

My home is in the Midwestern United States, but I also possess a deep love and appreciation for traveling the world and experiencing its beauty. Large towns and small, mountains and seas, trees, flowers, animals, great food, cultures, and amazing people, there is beauty all around us.

I am what could be called, 'a late bloomer'. Writing for career, friends, and family most of my life, I launched my published fiction career after my retirement. *"A Pineville Easter"* is my debut novel.

As a person, I am a firm believer in kindness and gratitude, and never ceasing to live while we are alive. I have found incredible joy in the last several years through avenues I never anticipated. I have found such excitement in 'retirement' that part of my personal mission is to encourage others to keep going while they can, and to make the latter half of their lives as fulfilling as the first.

You have many choices in what to read. I thank you for reading mine.

For more information on all Anne Fons things, I encourage you to visit my website at www.AnneFons.com.

In gratitude always,

Anne Fons